Ruby on the Outside

Ruby on the Outside

Nora Raleigh Baskin

Simon & Schuster
Books for Young Readers
New York London Toronto Sydney New Delhi

SIMON & SCHUSTER BOOKS FOR YOUNG READERS
An imprint of Simon & Schuster Children's Publishing Division
1230 Avenue of the Americas, New York, New York 10020

SIMON & SCHUSTER BOOKS FOR YOUNG READERS
is a trademark of Simon & Schuster, Inc.
For information about special discounts for bulk purchases,
please contact Simon & Schuster Special Sales at 1-866-506-1949
or business@simonandschuster.com.
The Simon & Schuster Speakers Bureau can bring
authors to your live event. For more information or to book an event,
contact the Simon & Schuster Speakers Bureau at 1-866-248-3049
or visit our website at www.simonspeakers.com.
Book design by Krista Vossen
The text for this book is set in Berling LT Std.
Manufactured in the United States of America
0515 FFG
2 4 6 8 10 9 7 5 3 1
Library of Congress Cataloging-in-Publication Data
Baskin, Nora Raleigh.
Ruby on the outside / Nora Raleigh Baskin.—1st edition.
pages cm
Summary: Eleven-year-old Ruby Danes has a real best friend for
the first time ever, but agonizes over whether or not to tell her a secret she has
never shared with anyone—that her mother has been in prison since Ruby was
five—and over whether to express her anger to her mother.
ISBN 978-1-4424-8503-7 (hardcover)
ISBN 978-1-4424-8505-1 (eBook)
[1. Mothers and daughters—Fiction. 2. Prisoners' families—Fiction. 3. Best
friends—Fiction. 4. Friendship—Fiction. 5. Aunts—Fiction.] I. Title.
PZ7.B29233Rub 2015
[Fic]—dc23
2014018268

For Jill,

because I followed her out of class,

in the early fall of 1979,

our freshman year at SUNY Purchase,

asked her if she wanted to be my friend,

and she said yes

Acknowledgments

Thank you to Charles Grodin for putting me in touch with Sister Tesa of Hour Children and for first making me aware of the serious issues facing incarcerated women today.

Thank you, Sister Tesa.

I couldn't have asked for more honest, intelligent, insightful, authentic, and generous voices than I got from Anthony Bautista, Kiki Leonard, Jeaniah Williams, and Theresa Warren. Thank you. Thank you. Thank you.

Huge gratitude to Kellie Phelan, who answered my endless questions and inquiries up until the very end of this writing process.

To Jenifer McShane, for making the very important documentary film, *The Mothers of Bedford*, and for her artistic encouragement.

To Emani Davis for spending time with me, sharing her life, and introducing me to the book, *All Alone in the World*.

To Alessandra Rose, who gets things done, and got me into the Bedford Hills Facility, which is no easy task.

To Rick Downey, supervisor of Volunteer Services at Bedford Hills for answering all my questions on the "inside."

To Nancy Gallt, Marietta Zacker, and to Kristin Ostby, and to everyone at S&S for believing in me and continuing to make my dream come true.

And as always and forever, to Steve, Sam, and Ben, with love.

Note: Any mistakes regarding the Bedford Hills Women's Correctional Facilities are mine alone.

Ruby on the Outside

Chapter One

It's all she's known her whole life, Matoo explains to her friends on the phone when she thinks I can't hear her. "Ruby doesn't remember anything different, so for her it's normal," she says about me.

But Matoo is wrong.

My dog, Loulou, might not know what it's like to walk off a leash, to walk free and choose where she wants to stop and smell and when she's done, and then decide for herself to mosey over to the next interesting spot and sniff, or not. She might not have any memory of running around outside without a collar around her neck. But that doesn't mean she *likes* it this way.

You can not know any better and still know you don't like something.

"C'mon, both of you," Matoo says to me and Loulou. "We've got to get back inside. It's so hot out here and I should start dinner."

I hate to do it, but I tug on Loulou's collar so she knows it's time to go in. She lifts her head and looks at me, because I am the one holding the other end of this leash. I am the one who can make her come when I want to, and she knows it. I'll never know what she's really thinking or what she smells in the grass, or those leaves, or the side of the building, but I can tell she doesn't want to go inside yet and I feel guilty making her.

Except it *is* hot out here, I do agree. And I am pretty hungry, come to think of it, so I give her little yank.

Loulou is straining her head toward some tuft of grass, locking her hind legs and gripping her claws into the ground so she can get one last, good inhale.

"Let's go, Loulou. There's nothing there," I say.

Nothing that I can see anyway.

But just because you can't see something doesn't mean it's not there. And just because you don't remember something doesn't mean you don't miss it. And just because you are used to something doesn't mean it's normal. So I give Loulou a little more time to sniff around and I know she appreciates it.

⁊

When I was little, I didn't understand. Every time we visited my mother in the Bedford Hills Correctional Facility for Women, I expected she was coming home with us.

"Not this time," my mother said. "But I'll be home soon. I promise. Soon."

So, I thought, *next time*. Next time is long enough to be soon. But each time, my mother said again, "Not yet. Not this time, sweetheart. But soon, I promise. Don't forget I love you. I will always be here for you. I will always be your mother."

I didn't know why she was saying that. Of course she was my mother. I just wanted her to come home already.

So maybe *this* visit was "soon" or maybe *this* was the time we would all walk out together. If not this week, then next, or the next. Or the next. After a while, Matoo started warning me before we even got inside, but I still didn't get it. We pulled into the parking lot, which looked pretty much like any other parking lot—if you didn't look up at the barbed wire—like a parking lot at the A&P and the one at the Petco and the one at the Home Depot.

Matoo said, "Ruby, Don't keep asking your mother when she's coming home. It's not nice."

I didn't understand.

How can wanting your mother to come home be not nice?

I wanted to hurry inside but a long line was forming by the visitors' trailer. My heart started beating faster, which is something my heart does whenever I am anxious about something, and right then, I was in a hurry about to get inside to see my mother. I tried reasoning with my own thoughts, to calm me down. Talking to myself.

It's okay. The line will move. No matter how long it takes. You will get to the front. No one will stop you from seeing your mom. And no matter how long it takes, she'll be waiting for you.

So my mind was talking, but my body did something totally on its own accord as if it was not listening at all. My heart started pounding harder. And then it was hard to breathe. The harder it was to breathe, the more my heart started to worry and beat faster, until finally I was wheezing and barely sucking in air, and my chest hurt. I reached up and took Matoo's hand, and at the same time, I willed my heart to slow and slowly the air made its way back into my lungs.

Finally, Matoo and I made it to the front of the line and inside the trailer, where there were seats, and even some old toys and books and all these posters on the walls with all sorts of encouraging sayings. Of course, I didn't call her Matoo back then. She was still Aunt Barbara. The line of people moved a little faster in here, and finally we made it inside.

We put all our belongings in a locker, showed our IDs. But we still had to go through all the security: the metal detectors, the wand search, the hand stamp, the gated doors, the big black bars, the hand stamp check, the sign-in, more bars, and finally we got to the visitors' room where we were assigned to a table.

That was hardest part. Waiting. Waiting again, with my heart threatening to start pounding again and my feet jittering. Sitting at our table with the big number twenty-eight marked on the top, watching everyone around us talking, laughing, hugging their mom, or sister, or daughter, while I was still waiting.

Matoo started to say something. "Ruby—"

She was going to warn me again. To be nice. Not to keep asking my mother when she was coming home.

"I know. I know," I said, because I wasn't listening to her. Because I had a plan.

"That's rude, Ruby. I am talking to you," Matoo said.

I sat up straight and listened, all the while going over my strategy silently in my head. I might have only been five or six at the time, but I was getting very good at living inside and outside my head at the same time.

Matoo was talking, but I could see the correctional officer sitting at her desk, way high up, at the front of the long visitors' room.

Some kids from a long time ago must have drawn that colorful picture they have covering her really tall desk, so the picture looked all friendly, but that woman sitting there was the boss of this room and everyone in it. She was the one who told everyone where to sit. And she was the one who asked people to leave when they were getting too loud or fighting. She was the one who told people when their time was up because other visitors needed to come in. And everyone did what she said, so I knew she was most certainly the one to ask.

She was the key player in my plan.

"Are you sure you are listening to me, Ruby?" Matoo went on.

I nodded. I folded my hands the way they taught me in kindergarten and waited.

I don't actually remember much of that visit except for the very end, when it was time to leave and my mother got that sad look on her face and I got that horrible stomachache. We had moved from the table into the children's center by that time—a little area that looks just like a nursery school, separated from the rest of the visitors' room by a wall of windows. Just before we were about to leave, I jumped up, pulled open the doors, and headed right for the big, tall platform where the officer in charge was sitting. Sometimes she came down from her post and walked around, but right then, she was sitting at her desk working on something, something I couldn't see because it was too tall. And she looked down at me.

"Please," I said. "Please, can I take my mommy home with me today? Please, I know it's been soon."

I talked as fast as I could, before Matoo could catch up to me, before anyone could stop me.

I went on, "I know because every time we come here, it's sooner, and now I want to take my mommy home with me. Please, can you tell my mommy it's soon now? Please, can you let my mommy come home with me today?"

"Whose child is this?" the correctional officer said. She looked as sad I was.

"Please, please," I cried. "I really want my mommy."

Then Matoo was there, pulling me back, trying to tell me something I couldn't understand. She was right next to me, but my mother was not. My mother stayed back at the table, because she wasn't allowed this close to the exit door. It was like there was something keeping her away from me, something invisible that only she could see. But just because you can't see something doesn't mean it's not there.

Because there was something about that place that made you just know that someone could stop you from doing whatever it was you were doing, at any moment, for any reason whatsoever. In this place, you couldn't go where you wanted to go. And you couldn't be where you wanted to be, until finally you stopped thinking it was possible.

But that didn't mean you liked it.

Chapter Two

No one in my whole fifth grade knows about my mother. I've kept that a secret and it hasn't always, or ever, been easy to do. There are so many things they tell you to ask your mother about when you are in school. I know they mean "either of your parents, or grandparents, or legal guardian" but most people, teachers included, just reduce that mouthful to "your mom."

Get your mom to sign this.

Ask your mother's permission.

Did you mother buy that for you?

Does your mother know you are eating that?

When people hear about Matoo they sometimes think I am Native American or African, which I can understand since that's what her name kind of sounds like. But it's nothing that interesting.

It's just Ma *T-o-o*. Or, more accurately, Ma *T-w-o*.

Like not my *real* mom, but my second mom.

"Mom Two" just sort of morphed into Matoo when I was starting school and it stuck because if I called her Aunt Barbara, or Aunt Bobbie, people always wanted to know where my mother was. But if I called her Matoo, they were confused enough not to ask.

Hopefully.

I've learned not to invite questions if I possibly can help it. So if someone wants to think I am a one-eighth descendant of the Iroquois tribe or from a long-lost Egyptian dynasty, I let them. It helps that I have long dark hair and brown eyes. But there is a girl who hangs out at the pool here who really does look like an Egyptian princess. I've seen her now two days in a row.

"Oh, that's Margalit something or other. They just moved to those units by the front entrance. You don't know her?" Kristin tells me. We are lying on our stomachs, on towels stretched out on the concrete by the pool. It is still a week before the end of school but summer is definitely here already.

Kristin was my friend from Mt. Kisco Elementary, but she is more like my condo friend because we aren't in any classes together at school. All the years I've been living here, from first to fifth grade, we never once ended up with the same teacher.

But Kristin and I come to the pool every sunny day after school when the weather is warm, and most cloudy ones too.

"No, I never saw her before," I say, but, of course, I had seen her.

Yesterday. I couldn't stop watching her. Kristin wasn't here yesterday. She was visiting her grandmother in Brewster, but Matoo and I were here. It was Saturday and boiling out even though it's only June, and the pool was packed but there was this girl. She was alone. The whole time I watched her, I didn't see her talking to anyone, not any other kid, not any parent or grown-up. But she didn't seem concerned with that at all. It's hard to say why, but I could just tell she seemed very comfortable being alone.

And that kind of intrigued me.

I watched her sitting on her towel in the grassy area reading a book. She was wearing a one-piece purple bathing suit with a green diagonal stripe from her shoulder to her hip. I couldn't see what she was reading, even though I tried to walk by on my way to the concession stand and get a peek. Whatever it was, it must have been good. She rarely pulled her gaze away from the pages.

And it was also kind of interesting the way she got

into the pool, swam around a little, like she didn't care if anyone knew she was there or not, got out again, and just walked back to her spot without wrapping a towel around her waist like a skirt. Lately, I feel naked when I get out of the water, like I have hide myself or at the very least, I walk really fast to get back to my spot and sit down. But this girl just strolled slowly like she wasn't worried about being seen or being seen not looking perfect, which made her look, well, look perfect.

But today, she is just reading a book and she hasn't gotten up once. I can only watch her from across the pool and wonder what she's really like.

"Margalit's a weirdo, so you're better off not knowing her," Kristin says.

I don't know where Kristin is getting her information, so I take it with a grain of salt, an expression Matoo uses.

"Ruby, you're not even hearing me."

Kristin is annoyed with me. "I was saying that Margalit's a weirdo, so you're better off not knowing her," Kristin tells me.

"Oh, sorry. I am listening. What did you say?"

But I'm not really that sorry, because a lot of the time Kristin is annoyed with me, which was another reason we probably weren't such good at-school friends. When Kristin had other choices, she usually chose someone else. But to tell the truth that was fine with me. Kristin was a little too close to my home life for comfort. I liked to keep school and home as far apart as I could.

On the other hand, Kristin is going away all summer to camp and I'll be all alone here. To top it off, this September I will be going into Fox Run Middle School and without a best friend, someone I can trust, well, I just have a bad feeling about it.

"I mean, just look at her. Don't even bother," Kristin says. "She's different."

"Oh, okay," I tell Kristin. "Thanks for warning me."

Now I am *really* intrigued.

Chapter Three

I've never intentionally missed a visit to see my mother. That's not to say there haven't been weekends we didn't get to go. Weeks we didn't get to go, or *couldn't* go, or someone was sick, or the car was not working, or there was a lockdown at Bedford Hills and we waited for hours and never got inside.

When she first went to jail, before her trial, before she got sent to Bedford Hills and we were still living up near Saratoga somewhere, I didn't see my mom for eight months. But since then I've never willingly turned down a chance to visit my mom, until just now.

Until today.

"I'm just thinking I can't go with you this time, Matoo," I am saying, but even as the words are coming out of my mouth I am regretting them. I feel bad already.

But I have to stay home today, because I know Kristin is going away again—she calls it a "play-date" which seems to be another mothery-type expression that never made its way into our house. And I am hoping that while Kristin is away, that girl Margalit will be at the pool and I'll get a chance to meet her.

"Well, it's visiting day and I'm just thinking you *are* going to come." Matoo is wiping out the top shelf of the fridge with a paper towel.

I am standing at the doorway to the kitchen watching her, and now I am really thinking hard. The air conditioner kicks on and the hum is like my brain working. I know I could just tell my mom the truth.

I can always tell my mom the truth.

And the truth is I've never had a real friend. A best friend, not just a condo friend. I think, partly it's because of my secret-keeping. I think the thing about having a best friend is that you don't have any secrets, at least not from each other. Most girls I know, and even boys I know, have one really, really important friend that rises above all the others who are just regular friends. It's the kid who always comes over after school. Sometimes they even have special sayings together. The boys make up crazy handshakes. The girls do each other's hair or dress alike on prearranged days and then act like it was just a coincidence because they are such good friends. There are two girls in my school who call each other "twins" even though they look nothing alike. They aren't even sisters.

So I know I could just tell my mom why I want to stay home today and she would understand. I just don't feel like explaining all this to Matoo.

So I almost start to tell Matoo that I have a big, huge book report due, which is the usual go-to excuse for everything, but then I remember it's nearly the end of June and a big, huge book report with a week left of school seems unlikely. The air conditioner shuts off as quickly as it went on, and the room is dead silent.

Matoo closes the fridge door and looks at me. "What is it?"

I saw something about migraines on television news this morning and it's the first thing that comes into my head, so I say, "I have a bad headache." And then, just to make sure, I add, "And I think I have a little stomachache."

Bad move. Matoo looks worried. Sickness is her best thing. She isn't so keen on things that hurt that you can't see, but she's really good at taking a temperature, spooning out cough syrup, or setting up the humidifier and filling it with that nasty VapoRub.

"Well, you know, it's going around. There's that summer virus. Or it may be food poisoning. Some kind of parasite. What did you eat yesterday?" Matoo says.

She looks really worried and I feel bad. Matoo lost her husband when she was younger and he was still young too. They had only been married five years and they never had any children. He died of a brain aneurysm so whenever someone has a headache I bet she thinks about her husband, Uncle Thomas. And now I feel terrible but not so terrible because maybe I think it is working.

"No, I'm not that sick," I say quickly. "Maybe I'm just tired."

"Ruby." Matoo is holding her glasses in her hand and rubbing the indent on her nose. Matoo wears thick glasses—really thick glasses. When she takes them off, there's a deep groove in the bridge of her nose.

I can't imagine holding up all that weight on my nose all day long. Maybe that's why she's always so worried. It's those heavy glasses.

"Maybe I should stay home with you," she says.

"No," I blurt out too fast. "I'll be fine. I'll just lie on the couch and watch TV. I mean, a little TV, and I'll read some."

I finally get Matoo to agree to leave me home alone, and then as soon as I watch her car pulling out of our spot in parking lot—space 102, like our house number—I really *do* get a stomachache, and it's a *horrible* stomachache.

I watch Matoo's car heading out of the condo complex without me and I am all confused. Maybe I should run out into the parking lot after her, but it's too late. I feel like I am losing my mother all over again. And there goes my heart, beating like crazy again. But I remember what my mother has told me: *We don't have so much time together, Ruby. So when we are together there is no pretending. I never want you to visit me and be wishing you were somewhere else. We don't have time for that. It just gives us more to talk about when you do come.*

So here I am, lying on my back, on my towel in the grassy area that surrounds the concrete ledge of the pool, trying to figure out how I can get to meet this new girl at our condo, when a shadow comes across my body. I feel the heat of the sun disappear from my face. I open my eyes.

"Hey, I'm Margalit. Wanna be friends?"

I sit up.

"Huh?"

"I'm Margalit. I see you watching me so I thought maybe you wanted to be friends."

"I wasn't watching you." It's a knee-jerk reaction.

She sits down on the edge of my towel. "Oh, well, I thought you were. I'm Margalit."

Today she is wearing a different bathing suit, a red one, like a lifeguard's but without the big white cross and without the wording. But you could get confused, I bet, if you were drowning or something.

"I'm Ruby Danes," I answered, not sure why I just gave my full name.

"Oh, cool," she says.

Then she falls quiet and that doesn't seem to bother her either, like it's just okay to sit here, so close to each other on my towel, and not talk, which I suppose it is.

Her black hair is wet and it shines, practically glistens in the sun. We sit like that for a while, and I am wondering if I'll just wait like this, watching this girl's hair dry.

"I'm hot," I say after another beat or two.

Margalit jumps up. "Great, let's go in the pool."

Chapter Four

I am pretty sure that this awful feeling I have, lying on the couch waiting for Matoo to get back from Bedford Hills, is what's known as extreme guilt. I also had to hide my bathing suit in my bottom drawer, turn on the water in the shower so it looks like I took a shower, because my hair is so wet and there's no way it will dry before Matoo gets home. Then just as I hear the front door lock turn I realize my hair will smell like chlorine anyway, and, oh, why didn't I just get in the shower and really wash my hair? Then I wouldn't be lying, at least, about one thing.

But it's too late.

"Ruby? I'm back."

Matoo walks into the living room and sits right down at the end of the couch. Maybe she doesn't smell anything.

"How was mom?" I ask.

Matoo shrugs.

"Did she ask about me?"

"Of course she asked about you. I didn't want to tell her you weren't feeling well. You know how upset she gets when she thinks you're sick."

Oh right, I didn't think about that. Why am I such a selfish person?

"What did you tell her?"

Matoo leans against the back of the couch.

"I told her you made a new friend at the pool and you wanted to hang out with her today."

What?

I look at Matoo to see if I can see anything in her face that might give her away, but her glasses are so thick, like prisms. I can't tell if she's tricking me.

Does Matoo know?

Did she know the whole time?

"I knew that would make your mother happy. She doesn't think you have enough friends," Matoo explains.

"Oh." That's all I say.

Talk about ironic. I can't now suddenly tell the truth and tell Matoo, *I do. I do have a new friend.*

But I *do*. I do have a new friend. At least, I think so. Margalit.

We spent a whole hour in the pool. First we had a

21

tea party under the water, holding our breath, crossing our legs, and sitting at the bottom of the shallow end, pretending to pour and sip cups of tea. To be honest, I'm not sure what the point of this was, but it was fun.

It was fun just being with someone who laughs so quickly and fully, like Margalit. I never laugh that easily, but with Margalit I was howling. Just hearing her laugh made me laugh, a deep, full laugh the kind that has a life of its own and feels like you are floating in a happiness tank.

Next we dove for dimes and nickels that I found in the bottom of my pool bag. We took turns being the one to throw the coins, scattering and waiting for them to sink.

"One, two, three, go," Margalit shouted and we both splashed into the water, trying to remember where we saw the money settle.

We did cannonballs off the diving board and did this made-up thing where we had to call out our favorite dessert in midair before we hit the surface of the water. We played all sorts of games that Kristin would have thought were too babyish until I said I had to get home.

"Why?" Margalit asked me. "It's still early. It's still hot out."

I had to go.

I had to get back before Matoo got home from visiting, but I said I could stay a little longer, and a little longer, and then it was almost four o'clock.

"I really gotta go."

Matoo never seemed to suspect anything. We eat dinner and I go to bed early. She comes in and sits at the end of my bed, like she has done every night since I told her my mother used to do that. The truth was, I had no idea if my mother used to do that or not, but it was one night, just a couple of weeks after we had just moved to Mt. Kisco and I was scared. It was a new house and I was starting first grade. I was already forgetting my mother, it had been so long, nearly a year since she was arrested, so I just said that. I didn't know how else to ask. I told Matoo, kind of offhanded like that—I think she was still Aunt Barbara back then—that my mother used to sit with me until I fell asleep.

Matoo was exhausted that night, I knew. She is a lot older than my mother, and besides she was still unpacking all our boxes and she had just started her new job and she probably wasn't used to having a little kid around all the time.

She sighed, but she didn't say anything and she sat down at the end of my bed. Matoo didn't sing or tell me a bedtime story, but she did sit there for a while, quietly, not saying anything. I remember that night, peeking every now and then to see if she was still there, and she was. Then, the next thing I knew, it was morning.

Now, all these years later and Matoo comes in every night and sits down. She doesn't wait until I've fallen asleep anymore, but she sits for just a minute or two. We usually talk about the day, school, chores, or what we have to do the next day.

"So are you feeling better?" Matoo is saying now.

I almost forget I am supposed to have a headache.

"Yeah, all better," I tell her.

Matoo is looking at me so I think it's because she can somehow tell if I still have a headache or not, just by looking at my face. But she says, "Why don't we get you a haircut?"

"A haircut?" I have been growing my hair for so long. My goal is to see if I can get it to reach midway down my back. Or does Matoo smell the chlorine after all and this is her way of punishing me for not telling the truth?

"Yes, a real haircut at a real fancy salon. You have such a pretty little face, you don't want so much hair overwhelming it."

No, this was just one of those times Matoo thinks she's forgotten something she is supposed to do as my stand-in mother. Matoo was not one of those ladies who gets her fingernails painted pink or her hair done once a week, but she thinks it's something a girl needs to learn about.

She means well.

"But I was wanting to grow my hair, Matoo."

"Well, we can talk about it in the morning." She pats my feet, poking up under the covers. She stands up. "Try and get some sleep."

When she closes the door I suddenly feel like crying. I miss my mother so badly and I missed my chance to see her today. I can't go back and fix it now.

My nose starts to tingle. I get this burning in my throat and I don't even know where it is coming from. I know I am lucky. I know I have a safe place to live and people who care about me.

I am ungrateful *and* a double liar.

Smile more, Matoo always tells me. *When you smile you feel better.* It's another one of Matoo's famous sayings.

So lying in the dark, I try to smile. I force my mouth to turn up at the corners. I think I am smiling and I wonder what my mother is doing. She is in her cell by now, the steel bars pulled shut and locked. Maybe she is asleep. Maybe she is thinking about me. I try to smile but I feel the wetness leaking out of my eyes and dripping down my cheeks onto my pillow. I miss my mother so much.

Chapter Five

Needless to say, the corrections officer didn't let me take my mother home, and "soon" became the most meaningless word in the world to me. It was six years ago that I tried to take my mother home with me, and after that, we all just stopped talking about it. We never used the word "soon" again, and in fact, thinking about it now, there are millions of things we just didn't talk about.

We didn't talk about those certain things but still, sometimes I would hear Matoo on the phone with my mother, or the two of them talking in front of me in clipped, cryptic sentences about things they thought I didn't understand. Parole hearings. Lawyers. Letters to some family named Tipps. Prisoner advocates.

And I was just as willing not to hear and not listen. And not to know.

I had figured out one thing very clearly that day: My mother was not coming home. And from then on, everything shifted from waiting to coping.

That same CO was still there. Not every time I visited, but a lot of the time. Enough that she knew me by name and I knew hers—Officer Monroe. She was actually the nice one. There was another semi-nice one, Officer Peterson. A meanish one, Officer Charles. And then there was Officer Rubins.

"Table fourteen," Officer Rubins told us one visit.

I didn't want table fourteen.

Table fourteen is right next to the vending machines and there's no privacy. But I didn't say anything. I must have been visiting my mother for a couple of years by then. And I may have only been seven years old, but I knew better than to make trouble. Matoo and I sat down and waited.

Sometimes it took a long time for my mother to arrive. Sometimes it took forever. They had to call down to the housing unit and my mother might not be ready. It wasn't like we were here for a doctor's appointment or a business meeting.

It was prison.

We just had to wait.

"She might be in the library or in her class," Matoo said. "Or on work duty."

My mother had a job in prison. She answered calls from people who thought they were calling the Department of Motor Vehicles and so when I was in school and had to tell someone where my mother worked, that's what I said. I told them she worked for the DMV, which really wasn't a lie at all.

I didn't mention that she got paid $1.10 an hour.

Matoo and I twiddled our thumbs, literally four fingers making little spinning windmills. There were books and toys in the children's center, but that part of the visitors' center hadn't been opened yet that day. The visitor's room was pretty empty still.

One by one, a few of the inmates had come down and those families were huddled together at their table. Each time the big metal door would clank open, everyone else would look up, hoping it was their person, finally coming in. I could hear that noise anywhere in the world and I would know what it was. My heart would stop and I would stop whatever I was doing, expecting to see my mother. It's that kind of sound.

That day, there was a little girl at the next table, a little younger than me, I guessed. She was waiting too. It looked she was with her grandmother, but the grandmother was just dozing, right in her chair, sitting up. They had been waiting longer than we had. Maybe the girl's mother was in her class or checking a book out of the library too.

Or on her work duty.

But then all of a sudden this girl made this funny noise, like a dog yelping or a cat when you step on its tail, but she didn't move; she sat frozen. I followed her eyes past the other tables, and all the other families, inmates in green and officers in blue, to where her mother had walked in.

The mom was so young and pretty. Her hair was twisted into tight braids that ended, each one, in a tiny colorful beads at the nape of her neck. And she was smiling, a smile bright with all the love in the world. Just like my mom did when she would see me waiting for her.

And for the first time, I wondered.

What could this pretty mother have done to be put in jail? In *prison*, because back then I didn't know the difference between jail and prison. It was all the same. On the inside. Or on the outside. You're either out or you're in.

Here.

Or there.

I knew as much about my situation as I wanted. I knew about my mother's husband, Nick. Even though we were all living together, I can't remember him at all. I had seen one picture of him, one that must have slipped by Matoo when she threw all the others away. He was tall and dark, with hair on his face but none on his head, and in the photo he is standing next to my mom, gripping her arm like he doesn't want her to get away. I don't know who took the picture, but she is squinting and he is wearing those aviator sunglasses. He looks very confident and I guess he was, because he convinced my mother to accompany him when he needed drugs and my mother thought she needed him.

So I never wanted to ask why my mother was in prison, but all of a sudden I wanted to know about this little's girl's mother.

What had she done? Did she have a bad husband like my mother?

"Larissa," the mother called out, and that seemed to do the trick; the little girl jumped right up out of her seat like a Ping-Pong ball smacked by a paddle. She ran directly to her mom. And I watched the mother wrap her two arms all the way around her little girl, until I couldn't tell one body from the other.

I don't remember anything about visiting with my own mom that time. I've had so many they start to blend into one another. But what I do remember was that when our visit was just nearly over, there was a random mandatory head count, or maybe it wasn't random. Maybe something had happened somewhere else in the prison. Whatever it was, everybody in the whole place needed to be accounted for.

All the visitors had to sit down, not move, and all the prisoners had to stop talking and stand.

"Don't move." Officer Rubins started counting with his little clicker everyone in green, everyone standing up.

It took another forever. Then, and no one said why, all the moms and sisters and daughters were all taken back to their cells and we had to leave. It was just one of those things.

"I'm just going to the ladies' room before we leave, Ruby," Matoo said. "Wait here."

I waited but I thought about that little girl again and I just had to know. I remembered her mother calling out her name—Larissa—and I took a chance.

"Can you tell me what did Larissa's mother did?" I stepped up to the CO. "Why is she in here?"

A lot of the correctional officers were women, but Officer Rubins was a man. He was tall, at least to me, and pretty fat. His face was all scarred with tiny indents. He never smiled, so I don't really know where I got the courage to talk to him at all. Just seven-year-old stupidity, I guess, combined with this strange new urge to find something out.

"Larissa's mother?" He looked down at me. I thought he was going to answer me. Maybe I had been wrong. Maybe he was nice after all.

"Yeah, the girl and her grandmother. They were sitting next to me and my mom. Table fifteen? Larissa. Do you know what her mother did to put her in jail?"

And Officer Rubins started laughing. His laugh was loud and like a bullet, it just forced its way out of his belly and his mouth and into my chest. When his laughing lessened to a chuckled, he just looked mean again.

"Never mind about Larissa's mother. Why don't you just worry about why *your* mother is here," he told me.

Of course, that's what I really wanted to know.

Of course.

But I wasn't ready for that. I wanted to keep my two worlds apart. I didn't want anything from this inside world that might affect my outside world. When I got home and *that* world became *this* world again. I decided to never make the mistake of asking about anyone else, ever again.

And then, hopefully, no one would ask about my mom.

Not even, and especially not, me.

Chapter Six

Visiting hours at Bedford Hills are from eight thirty in the morning to three thirty in the afternoon, which means during the school year I can see my mom only on weekends.

And now, even though school is out for the summer, I still have to wait a full week before I can see my mother again. During the week, I'm supposed to go to the pool, where two older kids in the condo run a "camp." The good news is that Kristin left for her real sleepaway camp in Maine or Maryland or Massachusetts—I wasn't really listening when she told me—and that Margalit gets stuck here with me and that Matoo seems to have forgotten about taking me to a fancy hair salon.

"This is so boring," I say. But I'm not really bored.

I am happy to be out of the house and happy that Margalit is here at camp with me. Happy it's not raining and it's not too hot. And happy that they have a carrom board.

So I'm not bored at all, but Kristin makes fun of me when I get too excited about things. So I think I have to act like I am.

"Really? I'm not," Margalit says. She is standing on the other end of the board getting ready to shoot her red checker piece into the hole, if she can. "I love carrom."

And, wow, that's so cool. But now I am feeling stupid for saying I was bored when I wasn't, and maybe that made her feel stupid, which makes me worried. I really want her to like me. I wouldn't want to hurt her feelings.

"Do you want to do something else?" she asks me.

She misses and it's my turn.

"Oh, no," I say quickly. "I love carrom too. I just thought you were bored. So I said I was bored. I know, weird, right?"

Margalit is just looking me. "No," she says. "Not weird at all."

I feel a big smile take over my face. Matoo might be right about smiling making you feel good. I look down at the wooden board, position my fingers, take my shot, and I miss too.

There are no cabins at this camp or dining hall or whatever else they probably have at real summer camps. We have the condo pool, a couple of high school girls from the condos as counselors, and the grass on the other side of the fence, where there is a picnic table, which is where we are having lunch.

"My mother made me peanut butter and jelly again," Margalit says. There are only five of us by noon. The one boy who comes usually leaves around eleven. I think this is more like a drop-off babysitting. It's not like we learn to make fires, sing camp songs, and roast weenies. Though I think that stuff might be fun too.

But right now it's me and Margalit, one really annoying seven-year-old girl named Elise, and our two "counselors," Beatrice and Yvette.

I have peanut butter and jelly too.

"Me too," I tell Margalit and we both open our mouths and bite.

"Beatrice is a funny name for a kid," Elise is saying to one of our counselors. Elise has finished her lunch, apparently. She gets one of those pack-aged lunches from the grocery store, with the little compartments of cheese or grapes and a container of milk, which Yvette keeps, as advertised in her flyer, in a cooler, which is never that cool, but Elise doesn't seem to mind, though. She doesn't seem to have eaten much of it.

"It's no funnier than Elise," Beatrice says. She's trying to have a high school–type conversation with Yvette, but Elise keeps interrupting.

"Yes, it is," Elise says. "It's like an old-fashioned name. Like an old-lady name."

"Gee, Elise. Thanks for that," Beatrice answers, but she doesn't turn her head. She and Yvette are both sitting on the same side of the picnic table, practically whispering to each other. When they talk quietly like this, they are talking about boys.

"Go finish your lunch." Yvette shoos her away.

"We'll go for a swim after rest time," Beatrice says and they go back to their whispers.

I think that Elise is going to start bothering *us* now, but she doesn't. She just looks kind of dejected. She gets up from the table and goes and slumps down onto the grass.

"I feel sorry for her," Margalit says.

"Yeah, me too," I say. "She's got no one her age to hang out with." But really that hadn't occurred to me until just then.

I know what it feels like to sit alone and feel left out, watching other kids hanging out with their best friends. But in this moment, now that I don't have to be doing that, I can see how sad that is for some-one else.

After we finish eating, Margalit and I are sitting under the shade of the one full-grown tree in the whole condo complex. It's a big, thick tree, with its root gnarled and poking out of the ground all around the base, like giant bark fingers. We each have our favorite "finger" to sit on and eat and talk.

We watch as Elise starts bouncing her pink rubber ball, the one she keeps in her pocket, on the con-crete. Elise and her parents live in the unit right next to mine. She is always bouncing that ball against her front steps.

"Too bad there aren't more little kids here for her to play with," I say. "She doesn't have any brothers or sisters, either, so she's alone all the time." I say this mostly because I want to look like I have something to offer, even if it's just how much I know about the neighborhood. Like maybe that'll be another benefit to being my friend.

Margalit looks at me with this sad face and I won-der what I've said wrong. It's just like me to say the wrong thing. I'm sure I have, but I don't know what it is.

"I used to have a brother," she says.

So now I know.

"Oh, I didn't mean like that. Like there is something wrong with that or anything. I mean, I don't have a brother or sister either." And now I am rambling because that's probably not at all what Margalit meant, but before I can fix it or make it worse or anything, she stands up and brushes the peanut-butter-and-jelly-sandwich crumbs from her shorts.

"Let's play another game of carrom before they make us rest on our towels." And she looks pretty happy again.

"Okay," I say. "Wanna ask Elise to play too?"

Margalit nods and smiles. "Yeah, that's a great idea."

Chapter Seven

I imagine there comes a certain time in a new friendship when the inevitable invitation comes up:

Wanna come to my house?

Which will mean, sometime fairly soon after that, you most likely have to reciprocate. This is exactly why I've always managed to successfully avoid it until this moment. Of course, that is also why I never had a best friend before.

"Wanna come to my house for dinner tonight?" Margalit asked me yesterday.

It isn't that I don't want anyone to come to my house. I do. It's just that I'm afraid they'll ask questions. They might wonder about Matoo's name or figure out that I am not, in fact, Navaho or Sioux or a descendant of any other Native American tribe. Or they will see the photo of my mother on the mantel.

It's actually a very important, special picture. It's a photo of me and mom at Christmas. But there are a lot of red flags in the picture. Well, not really red flags, but things that might lead to questions. Questions about where it was taken. And why it's so different looking.

They might ask.

For one thing, my mother is dressed in all green, but that, in and of itself, might not seem so odd. It's just a green sweater with the green collar of her shirt poking out and plain green pants. Her hair is pulled back in a ponytail, nothing fancy, and if you looked closely you'd see she has no jewelry on. But who would really notice that?

My mom is sitting on a metal chair—another giveaway—and I am standing in front of her, kind of between her knees. Her arms are around me. I am wearing this really ugly blue striped dress, because it's a holiday visiting day and they make a big deal of it at the prison, with decorations and sweets, and Matoo made me get dressed up for it with a hand-me-down dress from a friend of hers.

But that's not it either.

No, it's more about the roaring fireplace and the fur-trimmed Christmas stockings behind her. There is a big wrinkle right down the center, rolling right across the brick chimney and making a bump in that roaring fire, because it's really just a plastic background, like the screens they use for slide-show projections.

So it doesn't take a genius to tell it's fake.

There are no flames coming from that fire, no smell of cookies baking in the oven or turkey roasting. There were no presents under that tree. Not that year, the year before, or the year after. All of it was fake.

But then again, you couldn't get more real than spending Christmas Day with your mom in prison.

And I love that picture more than anything.

I just didn't really want anyone else to know about it.

Okay, so when Margalit asked me over to her house, I said no.

"Oh, all right," Margalit says.

Camp is over for the day. Yvette and Beatrice walk us all back to our houses. We drop Elise off first. When we get to Margalit's house, her mom is waiting outside the front door. At least I assume it's her mom. When you don't have a regular mom situation you'd think you wouldn't assume these kinds of things, but I usually do anyway. Just like everyone else does.

"Are you sure you don't want to come over, Ruby?" Margalit asks me again. Then she looks up at the mom, like maybe *she* could say something that would change my mind.

I look up the few steps leading to their house. But, oh no, that *has* to be Margalit's mom. She has the exact same black hair, shiny and straight, only the mom has hers wrapped up on top of her in that way that looks neat and secure but also loose and pretty.

When I visit my mom, she brushes my hair, sometimes for the whole visit. We aren't allowed to have a hairbrush, so she uses her hands.

"Now, Moo, don't put your friend on the spot," Margalit's mother says. "Maybe she needs to get home. Maybe she's just tired."

And I am so torn because Margalit is the first girl that ever seemed like she might be my real best friend and if I don't take this next step, I'll never find out. Next year is middle school, and by all accounts a best friend is an essential accessory. Not to mention, I really really like Margalit.

"Maybe another night," I say to Margalit, glancing up at her mom for her approval.

"How about tomorrow night, then?" Margalit jumps in right away.

Yvette and Beatrice are still standing there, waiting, not really listening but sort of half waiting for the conversation to be over so they can move on and get rid of me at my house, like when the bus driver patiently lets some kid hold on and say good-bye to his mom for longer than necessary. But you can bet if Margalit's mom weren't right here, Yvette and Beatrice wouldn't be being so patient.

"Moo, you're doing it again." Margalit's mother was going to start to protect me again, but time is running out, and we are only getting older and closer to sixth grade by the second, so I just say it.

"Okay. Sure. Tomorrow night."

Really fast, before I have a chance to come up with more reasons why this is a bad idea and change my mind, Margalit starts jumping up and down.

"Oh Mom, can you make us homemade macaroni and cheese? And can we bake cookies afterward and then do FIMO clay?"

"Okay, okay, hold on." She is smiling. "Ruby. It's Ruby, right?"

I nod.

"Well, first we'll have to ask your mom," Margalit's mom says. "Do you want me to call her?"

"Oh, no. That's okay," I say. "I'll ask her when I get home."

That's when Yvette seemed to come back to life.

"Okay, then," Yvette said. "All settled. Let's get you

home, Ruby. Bye, Mrs. Tipps. See you tomorrow."

Tipps?

Beatrice adds in, "See you tomorrow, Mrs. Tipps."

And somewhere in the back of my head that name sounds familiar, but I am more concerned with how I am now going to go to Margalit's house for dinner tomorrow afternoon without having to then invite her to my house, but maybe this will finally turn out to be my very first, very real best friend and maybe everything is going to work out perfectly.

Chapter Eight

It wasn't like we didn't have our own story. We did. Mostly, the story between Matoo and me about my mother, was to hate Nick Sands.

"I never liked him," Matoo would say. "Not from the first moment I met him. He wasn't nice to your mother. Oh sure, he said all the right things. 'Baby doll.' 'Beautiful creature.' He had all the lines, but that's all they were. Lines."

I can't remember my mother at all from our time with Nick. I liked to imagine her, though. I like to pretend. I have this movie in my head of the two of us living alone and I am just a baby. And because in order for a good fantasy to really work you need to weave in some factual details, we live somewhere outside of Albany. We live in a little house, one story, yellow with white shutters. Or sometimes it's red shutters because that part I have to make up. My mother makes pies for a living, which means she is in the kitchen all day and I get to play with pots and pans on the floor right next to her. She sings while she is cooking and at the end of the day, we eat pies for dinner, then she gives me a bath and brushes my hair with a brush, while she tells me a bedtime story about her own magical childhood.

I had to make that all up too.

I can't remember anything specific from before my mom went to prison. We don't talk about my real dad, but I know my mom was really young when she had me. So I think when Nick came around she wanted so badly for someone to love and take care of her, take care of *us*, that she would have done anything for him. At least that's how Matoo describes it.

The truth is, I didn't want to hear even that much. But sometimes, my mom tries to tell me things.

One visit, about a year ago, we were in the children's center, which is that separate area of the visitors' room at Bedford Hills. There are toys and stuffed animals and books and art supplies and posters, so when you are in there, you can almost pretend you are in a nursery school somewhere, instead of a prison.

I was curled up in my mother's lap, but I was leaning over the table drawing while we were talking. At ten, I was probably too big to sit like that, with all my weight on her legs, but she was holding me, balancing me while I was working hard in that coloring book, trying to stay inside the lines perfectly, trying not to make a mistake.

"The social worker wants me to talk to you, Ruby," my mother said.

I think it was the second time she tried to say this. I was trying to ignore her. I was glad I couldn't see her face, only the picture in front of me. Someone before me had already drawn in this coloring book. I found the only page that was still clean, that I could make my own.

"I mean, I want to talk to you too," my mom went on. "About what happened that night. About why I am in here. I think you are old enough now to hear some things."

I wasn't.

I kept coloring. Purple within the lines. Dark purple over the light purple.

And somewhere in my brain, a memory was triggered. There were little shots of bright white lights darting around a bedroom in my mind far away, flashlights and voices and shouting. And so long ago, a woman in a blue uniform handed me a teddy bear.

Then I don't remember anything else until I am living with Matoo, who isn't Matoo yet. She is my mother's older sister and I'd never met her before.

"I have to take responsibility for my choices, Ruby. I wouldn't be a good mother," my mother paused, like she was stopping herself from saying something and then with effort she continued. "I wouldn't be a . . . mother . . . if I didn't do that. If I didn't take responsibility."

I know Matoo says that my mother didn't do anything wrong. It was all Nick. I heard her talking, sometimes crying. Nick was a drug addict. My mother didn't even take drugs. Everyone gets tested when they get arrested and my mother didn't test positive for anything. Not even alcohol, and that's legal. She was in the wrong place at the wrong time. That's what Matoo says.

"Ruby? Are you okay?" my mother asked me.

I didn't want to hear whatever it was she was going to say. But I had to say something to act like I was interested and then get her to change the subject.

"What happened to him?" I picked out a new color, orange, and I started going over the parts I had already colored purple and the whole thing was looking like brown mush.

"To who?"

"Nick."

49

There were other kids around, some talking quietly, some playing games, some fighting with their mom, arguing about why they were getting in trouble in school or at home, or being disrespectful and angry. I never understood how you could use the tiny amount of time you have with your mom like that.

"He went to prison, Ruby. You never have to worry about him again."

"For longer than you?"

I wanted to believe there was something fair about this whole thing, that seemed so horribly unfair to me, but when I asked that question I saw Matoo rolling her eyes around in her head like she was having a seizure.

"What?" I asked.

"That doesn't matter, Ruby," my mother told me, which meant she wasn't going to answer me. "What matters is how I move forward from here and if you can forgive me."

"Forgive *you*?" My orange crayon snapped right in half in my hand. "For what?"

I watched as Matoo started shaking her head in some silent sister communication. "Let it be, Janis," she said finally.

And my mother got quiet. She kissed the top of my head, picked up a yellow crayon, and starting working on the page with me.

She was letting it go. Now I could breathe.

I already knew what happened to Nick, though, even before I asked. I had heard Matoo on the phone so many times even when I tried not to. Nick had some information about even bigger more dangerous drug dealers, the ones he bought drugs from, and he traded that information for a lesser sentence. He was offered what they call a plea bargain. He ratted out his drug supplier and in exchange he didn't have to spend as many years behind bars as my mother, who had done nothing. She didn't have anything to give them in exchange for a lighter sentence. They didn't even offer her a plea bargain.

Nobody needed anything from my mom.

But I did.

Chapter Nine

Margalit's house looks almost identical to mine. The bedrooms are in the same place, the same little balcony from the upstairs overlooking the living room. The fridge and the stove and the sink are all in the exact same place as ours, but hers is ten times more crowded. And it's not just because three people live here instead of just two—Margalit, her mom, and her dad, who I haven't met yet—it's all their stuff.

I've never seen so much stuff. So much cool and interesting stuff. There are things everywhere, ceramic bowls filled with coins or dried flower petals, one with glass marbles. There are books, just randomly piled or stacked on top of any sort of surface; magazines; a little collection of antique-looking wind-up toys. Colorful glass bottles are lined up on the windowsill in the lower-level living room.

Matoo likes to keep our house very neat. If she sees me get up from an upholstered chair in the living room, she runs over and smooths out the lines in the fabric so you can't see that anyone had ever been there. We have a glass table, so you don't have to worry about your drink leaving a stain, but we aren't allowed to have any drinks in the living room, so it stays pretty clean.

It's not that Margalit's house isn't clean. It is. It's just wonderful. The white walls are so covered with artwork, framed and unframed, that there is hardly any white you can see. Some of the paintings were done by Margalit's mother and some by their grandfather, I am told, as Margalit points everything out and explains it. The couch is all mushy and soft looking, and there are different-colored, different-size pillows just thrown all over it, not fluffed up at all. Some are downright smushed to smithereens.

Matoo wanted to know whose house I would be eating at and what time I'd be home, but other than that I think she was happy I was eating with a friend. *Remember to smile*, she told me, *and be polite.*

I am smiling now.

"I hope you like my homemade macaroni and cheese. I didn't think to ask," Margalit's mom is saying when the house tour brings us into the kitchen. "Not everyone loves it like Moochie here does."

That's what Margalit's mom calls her. Moochie. Or just Moo.

"Oh, I love it," I answer, though I've never had homemade and I am wondering if it will be as good as the kind from the box, because I see it in the baking dish and it isn't even orange. Then Margalit pulls me by my arm.

"Come see my room," she says.

We are both sunburned from being outdoors all day. Yvette wasn't there today and Beatrice kept us at the pool all day. She was actually a lot more fun without Yvette around. I guess, Beatrice felt she could be more like a kid without Yvette around. We played Marco Polo and water tag and it was almost like we were just four friends. I even think Elise had a good day.

I follow Margalit up the stairs, which are just like my stairs, and into her bedroom, which is right where my bedroom would be.

"Wow," I say. It's all I can say.

Wow.

Before we can even walk into the room, we have to get past all the loose scarfs, hanging like a soft wavy rainbow from a bar that stretches across the top of the doorway. I carefully move some out of the way and then I kind of have to duck to get inside.

"Wow." I say it again.

Margalit has a big double bed, like grown-ups have, but it's anything but grown-up looking. Like her couch downstairs, her bed is covered with pillows, but it is also covered with stuffed animals and blankets that look like they might have been baby blankets, knitted and flowery. One cottony blanket bunched up at the bottom has blue bunnies on it. There is one big sort of pillow–stuffed animal combo and it looks really old, and really well loved.

Her walls are covered with posters, some that were clearly from kindergarten, like Hello Kitty, and some must be pretty new, like Demi Lovato. Margalit's room is just like she is: a free spirit. An open book. An open heart with lots of color.

And then there are her books. Everywhere. Her shelves are filled with what looks like a history of art projects—little FIMO-clay creations, beads, crepe paper flowers—and her books are stacked on the floor, under the bed, and on the windowsill.

It takes me a while to see everything.

"My mom keeps wanting me to clean up," Margalit says. "I will. Soon."

"Well, it's not dirty," I say.

Margalit bounces on her bottom right onto her

bed. "Thank you," she says. "That's what I say."

"And it looks like you've lived here forever," I say, because it does. It is so full of Margalit.

"I know, my mom wanted me to, but I wouldn't get rid of anything when we moved here from Glens Falls."

"Where's that?" I ask, not because I really want to know but it sounds polite. I want so much for Margalit to like me. I don't want to do or say anything thoughtless or rude by mistake. Sometimes I do that. I don't mean it, but I do.

"Oh, it's a little town upstate. Near Saratoga," she tells me

Saratoga?

That's where we used to live and I am just about to tell her that but I'm not sure that's very interesting, or if that's like being one of those friends that whenever you tell them something they tell you something about themselves right away. So I can't decide, but I don't have to because right then her mom calls up the stairs telling us dinner is ready.

"We gotta wash up." Margalit jumps to her feet. "I can't wait for you to taste my mom's cooking."

Me neither.

And by the way, homemade mac and cheese is much better than the kind from the box. Dinner is delicious. I wasn't going to ask, but Margalit's mom asks me if I want seconds, and I do. Margalit's dad is working late, so I don't get to meet him.

It's only seven thirty and it's still light out. Matoo had said it was okay for me to walk back home by myself. It's just two rows and a few condos down. But Margalit's mom makes me call my house first to say I'm on my way. I even remember to thank Margalit's mom for dinner before I leave.

"Anytime," she says.

Margalit echoes, "Anytime."

Now Matoo is waiting in the doorway. The light in the hall is on behind her and she's almost glowing. Her hands are on her hips.

"What's wrong?" I ask. I stop at the edge of the sidewalk, the way Loulou does when she doesn't want to come in from her walk, when it's so nice out and there's so much more of the world to explore.

"Nothing, why do you think something's wrong?" Matoo steps out of the way as if that will encourage me to come in faster. She takes off her glasses and rubs her eyes.

"I don't know," I say, but I still haven't moved closer. "You look mad, that's all." Without her glasses, Matoo looks more sad than upset, actually. Her face looks smaller. Her worry is more visible.

"Come on, come on already." She puts her glasses back on and starts waving her arms. "You're letting all the bugs in."

When I get inside, I see a bowl in the sink with left-over milk and a few Cheerios still, which Matoo must have had for dinner. I can't believe she hasn't washed her dishes yet and put them away.

Something *is* wrong.

"Did you have a good time?" she asks me.

"Oh, yeah. I had a great time," I say. "I really did."

Matoo smiles at me. "I'm so glad," she says. Her face relaxes.

I know it sounds crazy, but I think Matoo missed me tonight. Like maybe she likes it when I mush up her pillows.

"Next time, you can invite her here."

I think I will.

Chapter Ten

It's pouring rain. Yvette and Beatrice can't believe we showed up this morning for camp—me and Margalit. So far no one else has, which at this point just means Elise.

It's dark inside the clubhouse, which is our rain-day location, but I don't think anyone thought we'd really use it because it's pretty dingy. What it is, is a big empty room they use to store pool stuff over the winter, so it is filled with extra folding chairs, tables, hoses, rakes, and umbrellas stacked against the walls, and there is a steady drip of water in three places, plunking down onto the concrete floor.

"Okay, guys," Beatrice is saying. We have fitted ourselves all onto one big beach blanket with another towel on top of that, so even in this damp weather it's actually warm and cozy. "This is what we're going to do."

That must be her cue, because Yvette dumps out a big white plastic bag from Target; notebooks, colored pencils, markers, pens, little-kid scissors, and glue sticks all spill out. Seeing it all, I can feel my skin tingle and my heart thumbing a little bit faster. It's exciting, all those brand-new art supplies and before I can stop myself I blurt out with unbridled enthusiasm, "Oh, I love colored pencils!" and I instantly feel my face heat up with regret.

I've done this before—just this past school year, in fact, in fifth grade. It was early in the school year. It was our first year moving from classroom to classroom, but just one switch. Math and science with Mr. Williams and then right across the hall for social studies and language arts with Ms. Genovese. My embarrassing display of eagerness happened to occur in Mr. Williams's class.

We had just learned about the seven characteristics of a living thing. First, Mr. Williams asked everyone, or anyone, to guess. I think making kids guess always spells trouble and I don't know why teachers haven't figured this out. It's not like it makes everyone think or figure things out for themselves, it just creates chaos.

But anyway, after a few really ridiculous answers and a lot of toilet jokes from the boys, Mr. Williams wrote all seven characteristics of life on the board one by one explaining about each one: organization, reproduction, energy, response, growth, and adaptation. And without meaning to, I started thinking about my mother because there was something missing from that list, but I didn't want to share it out loud.

Eating is swell. Growing up, maybe. Adapting and being able to figure things out on your own is pretty crucial too, I suppose.

But love, I was thinking. *Living things need to be loved.*

Well, maybe not all living things, like maybe not amoebas or earthworms, but human beings do. Human beings need to be mothers who love their children, and children need their mothers to love. I'd read about babies in orphanages who actually don't grow because no one picks them up and loves them.

So my mind was wandering and I wasn't really listening and then all of sudden I noticed that the class is talking about manatees and baby seals and I didn't want to be thinking about my mother and how I can't be with her, so I just blurted something out.

"Oh, I love manatees!"

And the whole class got quiet and it wasn't because I'd just said something really stupid. It was because I seemed so happy about it, too eager to share, like a little kid, and that made everyone uncomfortable and they all started laughing.

They started laughing *at me.*

And I slouched down in my seat and vowed never to look overly excited about anything again.

But now I feel the same embarrassment heating up my face, only this time, instead of laughing at me, Margalit says, "Oh, me too. Don't you just love a brand-new perfectly sharpened pencil?"

She takes one of the colored pencils out of the box and holds it up.

"Good for both of you, then," Yvette is saying. I think she is being sarcastic, but I don't even care.

"This long, long day should go just swimmingly then," she adds.

Beatrice laughs like that is really funny and they both get up, head over to take down a couple of folding chairs, and start their high school–type conversation.

They leave us alone. The rain is steadily hitting the roof of the clubhouse, like hundreds of tiny drummers. The wind picks up. The rain shifts direction and smacks against the Plexiglas windows.

"Let's write a story together," Margalit says. "And draw pictures to go with it."

"Okay." I like that idea. I've never written a story with someone else before, but it sounds like fun. I pull out one of the spiral notebooks. Margalit does the same.

"I'll start drawing first and you start writing and then we'll switch," she says.

I look down at the blank pages, tiny blue lines inviting me to touch my perfectly sharpened pencil right down between them and see what story is left behind.

"What do I write about?"

"Anything you want," Margalit tells me. "So what should I draw? Let me think about it."

I'm sure it's raining in Bedford Hills, too, and that thought comes into my head but I know if my mother is in her cell, she can't see it. I wonder if she can hear it. I wonder if there are other ways to know if it's raining. Can she hear it? Do the COs come into work and talk about the weather? What is it like not to see the sky when you wake up in the morning?

The bright, beautiful sun or the dark, stormy clouds. The soft humid breeze on an early July morning. The misty cool breeze of a summer storm.

It's just so sad, so I blurt out, "Manatees?"

Jeez, that was stupid, but I need something to fill my head.

"Perfect," Margalit says. "Did you know that they think maybe early explorers, like even Columbus, thought that the manatees were mermaids swimming in the ocean?"

"Mermaids?"

"Exactly," Margalit says.

So I say, "I'll write a mermaid story."

"And I'll draw a mermaid and I'll throw in some manatees."

Margalit holds up her notebook. She has already begun decorating the cover. "This will be our illustration book and the one you've got can be our storybook."

We worked all morning and all afternoon, trading back and forth. I started a story about a mermaid and a manatee. Then I passed it on to Margalit and she wrote a little bit more while I drew a picture to go with the part I had just written. I didn't think too much about it. It is pretty much like playing house or playing dolls, only instead of setting up toys I just wrote down what I imagined everyone in the story was doing and what they were saying. We worked on our story and illustrations all the way through lunch.

Eating while we work. And just like that, the time goes by. It's three o'clock and the sun comes bursting out. Yvette pulls open the sliding door and we all stand looking out, the sunlight glistening and sparkling off every wet surface, every leaf and blade of grass—even the plastic lounge chairs that are set up around the pool are shining.

"Oh great, *now* it gets nice out," Beatrice says. We all emerge from the clubhouse and outside into the fresh air.

"I think I lost half my tan today." Yvette holds out her arms.

I am blinking in the light. It feels like we've been underground for weeks and that we've just lived a whole other life, the life Margalit and I wrote down in our storybook and illustrated.

"We need a title," Margalit says. She's rubbing her eyes.

"Yeah, we do."

Even Yvette and Beatrice get in on the discussion as we all walk back to our houses, but we haven't come up with the perfect title yet.

My sneakers get wet because instead of staying on the paved sidewalk Margalit and I keep running around each other on the grass.

"My toes are squishing in my soaking socks," Margalit says.

"Mine too."

And this seems to launch us into a whole other conversation about wrinkly toes and fingers and memories of staying in the bathtub too long. Yvette and Beatrice aren't the least bit interested but Margalit and I seem to be at no loss for things to add to the infinitely engrossing discussion.

"To be continued," Margalit says when we get to her door. "Hey! Hey, let's never say good-bye to each other. Let's always just say, *To be continued*."

"To be continued," I answer.

"Oh, and hey, wouldn't that be a great title for our story? *To Be Continued*, because we can keep writing forever. The never-ending story. We can just go on and on."

Even Yvette and Beatrice approve.

"To Be Continued," I repeat.

And I *know* I have a real best friend.

Chapter Eleven

I almost had a best friend once before. Tevin. I know that's a boys' name because Tevin *was* a boy, but it was a while ago, like last year when we were still little.

Back then you could be friends with a boy—best friends, even. He lived in New York City and we met at Bedford Hills. The whole time in line, I kept noticing this same boy, taller than me, but I could tell he was about my age, ten. I had been coming to visit my mother for years already and I could tell he was a newbie.

When we got to security, they wouldn't let Tevin come through the metal detector with his miniature action figure. You can't bring in anything. Not anything. Sometimes they send you back just because of what you are wearing.

Once I saw a woman drive ten hours just to get turned away because of her shoes.

"There's a Target right down the road, miss," the corrections officer tried to tell her. But this woman got really angry and that just got her kicked out completely.

Imagine coming all that way to see your mom, or sister, or whoever she was coming to see, and wearing the wrong shoes?

No sandals allowed. No tank tops. No short shorts. No backless shirts or dresses. I saw a woman made to change because the neckline of her blouse was too low. And they don't like T-shirts that say bad things or anything they don't like. It's up to them. No use arguing. Arguing is not allowed either.

But Tevin wasn't arguing. He just didn't understand what was going on. He had a little Batman toy in his pocket, and they wanted him to put it in the locker before they would let him through.

Tevin started crying, right there in line, and that's when I knew for sure this was his first time. On the outside, it would have been pretty bad for a boy to cry in public like that, but in here, we all understand, and no one even looks at you sideways if you're crying.

One time or another, everyone on the inside cries.

And I knew that feeling Tevin was having. You get stuck on one little thing, and all of a sudden it becomes the most important thing you've got, and you don't want anyone to take it away from you.

It's like they'd already taken away the most important in your whole life—your mom—and then they wanted this, too. They wanted this stupid little action figure. Or whatever it happened to be. It didn't make sense, but I knew what he was feeling.

"It's okay," I walked over and told him. "Everything stays safe while you are visiting your mom, and then you can get it back again when you leave."

There was a long line behind us and people were getting a little annoyed, but not too much. That's one thing about Bedford Hills—everyone is here for the same reason, and everyone here has some heartache and some secret that no one else but someone in here could ever understand.

And even though lots of other grown-ups had told him the exact same thing, Tevin just nodded his head at me and he let me help him.

"The locker thing is kind of cool. Do you have a quarter?"

He shook his head no.

"Here, I've got an extra one." But I didn't, and Matoo knew that, but she let me give him my quarter anyway. I showed Tevin how to put it in the slot and turn the key.

"Just don't forget your locker number, that's all you have to do. Fifty-two. Got it?"

Tevin nodded again and then he said, real quietly, "But I just bought this and I wanted to show it to my mom."

I straightened up my shoulders and started to tell him something, something like a teacher or a CO would say: *Well, we can't all get what we want, can we?*

But I didn't say that.

"I know," I said. "It stinks. But it'll be okay. I promise." *Promise?*

Of course, what could I promise?

Nothing.

Tevin and I seemed to show up on the same days and about the same time, and after a few months, I started expecting to see him. Sometimes, when there was a really long wait outside the trailer we would break away from the line, take a little walk along the fence and talk. I didn't ask, of course, but Tevin told me about his mother.

"She shouldn't be here," he told me. "She didn't do anything."

I had long since stopped thinking like that. I knew

my mother too had been in the wrong place at the wrong time. She made some bad choices and now we were "all paying the price." But like Matoo liked to say: *It doesn't help to dwell on it. It's in the past,* she would say, ever since that day my mother tried to talk to me. I don't want thoughts like that in my mind.

We need to move on, Matoo would tell me. *Let it go.*

"I know," I told Tevin.

"No, I mean it," Tevin insisted. "It was this lady who moved in next door to us. She didn't have a car, but we did. I don't know how she got around or anything. We used to see her walking and sometimes my mom would drive her to the grocery or stuff like that, but this one day, I wasn't home. If I was home it wouldn't have happened. But I wasn't home. That's why it's my fault. I was at the movies with my stepbrother, but I should have stayed home. I didn't even want to go. If I had been home my mom wouldn't have given that lady a ride to her uncle's."

Tevin was talking really fast and I could tell he was trying not to get too mad. Too upset. Or cry. "That's what she told my mom. She just needed a ride to her uncle's. That lady didn't even have an uncle."

Tevin's mom had only been in prison for a few months. He'd get used to it, I thought. You have to make it through that whole first year. That's what everyone says. First you have to survive one year, your birthday, their birthday, a Thanksgiving, a Christmas, one of every holiday. Tevin needed more time, a full year.

"It's not your fault," I told him because that's what grown-ups always say. So I said it.

He'd be okay. He just needed to talk.

"It wasn't her uncle. It was a drug dealer," Tevin went on. "And the police were there waiting, and then they found out that the lady had a gun. My mother didn't know that. She was just doing that a lady a favor, but no one believes her."

I didn't know what to say.

"She didn't even know the lady. She got ten years for the drugs and two more for the gun. My mother never did drugs. She didn't have a gun and now I don't have a mother. I didn't have a father to begin with."

Listening to him, I was just thinking how people here are just like me, and how nobody on the outside is like us at all. And how it's like there are all these voices and no one is listening. So I tried to listen really hard, because there wasn't anything else I could do.

"I'm going to get her out of here," Tevin was saying. "I'm all she has and I have to."

I knew she was all Tevin had too.

Then every time I saw Tevin he would give me

updates about his mother's chances for a retrial and his whole family's letter-writing campaign. I didn't once think about why we weren't doing that. I just listened. Tevin got better and better at understanding the whole process. He might have been ten years old, but he sounded like a lawyer.

One time he brought me photographs to show me before we got into the security area. He always brought his own quarter now.

And then one day when he got up to the counter to check in they told him his mother wasn't there anymore. Matoo and I were right behind them in line when the corrections officer said, "She's been transferred."

It was the first time I heard Tevin's grandmother speak. "What?" she asked. "What? Where is my daughter? What do you mean 'transferred'? When did this happen? Why weren't we told?"

Tevin was quiet. He looked like all the air had been sucked right out of him. But he was still standing up.

The officer at the desk checked his list. "Albion," he said.

I knew what that was. Albion was the only other state prison for women in New York. It was really, really far away, almost in Canada. Sometimes women went there right before they were going to be let out. So maybe it was a good thing.

But Tevin wouldn't look at me. He didn't say a word. He and his grandmother had to step out of line and me and Matoo were next. I never saw Tevin again and I had no way to find him. I never thought to ask him his last name or his address or his e-mail. It never crossed my mind that he wouldn't just be here, every week, just like me.

But he was gone.

I liked to believe that Tevin's mother had a new trial and they found her innocent and they all went home from Albion together. Like a magical storybook with a happy ending.

I like to believe that.

Chapter Twelve

In a way, after I was done being sad about Tevin, I was glad Tevin was gone, because he made me think too much.

Why do some people go to prison and some don't?

Do they put people in prison so they can't hurt other people?

Or do they put people in prison to punish them?

Or do they put people in prison so they have time to figure out what they did wrong so they can change? And if that's the case, how does it help to take a mother away from her child? A child away from his mother?

But now I have a best friend, Margalit and the hardest stuff we have to think about is what's going to happen next in our story. So even though I haven't forgotten about that other stuff, my brain gets a little time off.

"I think we need to work on it at my house tonight," she is telling me.

It hasn't rained again, but a lot of our outdoor time we spend on our stories, sitting under the umbrella table by the pool, while Yvette and Beatrice talk or try to teach Elise how to swim. That one boy who used to come hasn't come back. Guess he felt outnumbered.

Margalit and I finished our mermaid story and now we are working on a fairy story about two elves that get into all sorts of trouble. I figured out the fun of this game is to throw Margalit some twists and turns and surprises in my chapter that she has to figure out in her part, and still make the story make sense and have that *So what?* like my language arts teacher, Ms. Genovese, would say when we study writing in class, like *That's an interesting series of events, but so what?*

The *So what?*

We want our story to have a meaning.

Margalit wants me to come to her house again so we can continue work on our elf story, but I still haven't had her over to my house yet.

I am thinking that if Margalit is really my best friend, I should tell her the truth. I should tell her about my mother. Because I'm pretty sure Margalit thinks that

Matoo is my mother, and it's not that I don't like Matoo—I love Matoo—but she is *not* my mother.

I feel like I can trust Margalit. I feel like there isn't anything I couldn't tell her.

Besides, Matoo was the one to suggest I invite Margalit over. So I say out loud, "Why don't you come to my house this time?"

Margalit looks excited. "Okay, we can just stop at my house and ask my mom. But don't you have to ask your mom first?"

Now, there's a question. I know no one would believe me, but I've never had anyone over to my house for dinner before, so I wasn't sure what I was supposed to do.

"No, it's fine. She"—I just say "she"—"loves it when I bring people over."

Which is kind of true, because I know Matoo would love it if I had a friend, but as I am talking, I also know Matoo hates surprises.

But as it turns out, it's all fine. No worries. We stop first at Margalit's house after camp and Margalit's mother calls my house and makes sure it is okay, and Matoo happens to be in a particularly good mood. She says she'd be "thrilled to meet my new friend." We practically skip the rest of the way, with Yvette and Beatrice trailing behind.

☙

My room isn't anywhere near as fun or interesting as Margalit's, but she acts like it is.

"Oo, I love your desk."

I turn my head to see what she is talking about. My desk looks pretty average: wood, with drawers on either side, and a chair pushed neatly underneath.

"It's so clean. You must take your homework seriously. It looks like a high school desk."

I ponder that. I guess I do take my schoolwork pretty seriously. My mother asks to hear about my homework every time I see her. She asks about all my tests, and even if it's been a couple of weeks, she remembers everything. She even gets special permission from the social workers to talk on the phone to my teachers if she thinks they need to hear something about me. I've gotten the same message all my life from my mom:

Do well in school.

Don't get into trouble.

Make smart choices.

Don't grow up to be like me.

"So you're a really smarty pants, then, right?" Margalit asks me, and I know she's not making of fun of me. She's impressed and she sits down at my desk like she's testing it out.

"I guess so. I get really good grades." I can feel myself blushing a little. I think this is a good time to come clean. Not that I've been lying exactly but before we go downstairs and eat, before she asks me why I call Matoo "Matoo," or before she sees that photo on the mantel, I should tell Margalit the truth.

"I wish I got better grades," Margalit is saying.

She sits down on my bed and Loulou jumps up next to her. "And you are so lucky to have this cute dog. You must be really smart in school. Maybe we can study together in sixth grade."

Margalit is petting Loulou and I get this funny feeling there is something she is trying to tell me, too, because she is talking so fast.

"I mean, I do okay in school, but I think my brother got all the brains and didn't leave any for me," Margalit says.

She is being so nice and so open about herself that I might have to interrupt and tell her flat-out:

My mother is in prison.

The truth floats over my head like a cloud that follows me everywhere I go. It's dark and heavy. It won't go away if I talk about it but it will be easier to carry.

But Margalit keeps talking and I can't find a place to butt in.

She is fiddling with the pencils that are stored in

a special pencil holder on my desk. I made it in the children's center. Margalit goes on. "I could probably do better actually, but I think my parents like remembering my brother as the smart one, you know what I mean? Like that's how things are supposed to be. I am the artistic one. He was the smart one."

She turns to face me.

I want to say something, because I can tell I am supposed to, but I really *don't* know what she means.

"Is that your brother you told me about?" I ask. I remember she told me that she *used* to have a brother, but I've seen lots of kids with lots of different stories. Kids with parents they had and then didn't, kids that didn't have parents and then they come back, brothers and sisters they didn't know they had, or had and then didn't.

I wonder if I should have known, if I should have seen his room or heard her talking about him before, but I just wasn't listening good enough.

Then Margalit tells me, "Yeah, Josh. Well, Josh was my older brother, but he died a long time ago."

"Your brother?" I say. "Your brother's name was Josh?"

"Yeah," Margalit says. "He was twelve years older than me. I know that's a big difference. My mom tells me they had Josh when they were so young, like he was a mistake, but I think it's probably the other way around. I never talk about it. You're the first friend I've ever told."

Josh?

Tipps?

"You're my first real best friend, you know," Margalit says. "I'm so glad I could tell you all this."

"You can tell me anything," I say.

And something tells me not to say anything about my mother right now. Not yet. Something inside just tells me to stay quiet.

"Let's go down and see if dinner is ready," I say, but my brain is saying something else, quietly working in the background.

And once my brain starts thinking like that, I worry nothing good is going to come of it.

Chapter Thirteen

I still have that teddy bear, the one the woman police officer gave me the night my mother was arrested. I don't touch it, but I can't bring myself to get rid of it. It's still got the stiff red ribbon tied around its neck. I don't think Matoo knows why I have a teddy bear on my top shelf. She, of course, wasn't there that night, so I don't have to explain it to her. We lived in Saratoga back then. I don't even know where Matoo lived. I didn't ever see her back then. I didn't even know I had an aunt until they took my mother away.

I was only five years old.

I remember a few things, like remembering a movie you saw a long time ago that you weren't paying too much attention to in the first place. Still, sometimes, in the dark, against my will, when I am just trying to fall asleep, snapshots start coming into my head.

Nick and my mother were fighting. I could hear them from my bed. I didn't think much of it. I mean, I hated it, but they fought all the time. The scary part was if Nick lost his temper, if he broke something, or grabbed my mother's arm and left his fingerprints as dark bruises on her skin, and I would hear her crying.

But that night, after the yelling stopped, it just got quiet.

When I heard my mother's footsteps coming near my door I quickly turned my head to the wall and pretended to be fast asleep. I could tell she was looking at me, listening. I tried to make my breathing slow and even. She walked away from my bed, out of my room, and she carefully closed the door behind her.

A few seconds later I watched the car lights move across my ceiling and down my wall, I knew they had driven away.

I wasn't afraid. Not really. I was tucked into my bed. Safe in my room. The door was closed.

I waited.

And I waited.

I must have fallen asleep because the next thing I remember is the sound of our front door cracking off its hinges—splintering, cracking, breaking, booming shattering—the men's voices, and the bright lights shining under my bedroom door. The sound of things falling, drawers opening. I could hear it. I could hear walkie-talkies and shouting, footsteps. Voices that weren't my mother's. And weren't Nick's.

I froze. Every sound shot through my body, sinking me deeper and deeper into my covers. I was alone.

I was alone.

Then my whole room lit up when my bedroom door flew open.

"It's okay, sweetheart." A woman's voice. "It's okay." The woman policeman handed me the teddy bear and nothing was okay. Ever again.

Then everything is pretty much a big bank of fog, until I remember living with Matoo here in the condos in Mt. Kisco, and I had no idea how either me or my stuff got there. It's like there's a big chunk of time that just disappeared. I suppose for a while we were all lost and then slowly, slowly it just started to be home. I didn't ask any questions but I was vaguely aware that being here had something to do with being near my mother so we could visit her easily—so when she came home we were ready.

Soon.

And when "soon" never happened, the past fell

away, along with all those meetings, and phone calls, lawyers and plea bargains, court dates, babysitters, more meetings, more phone calls, another trial date. A new lawyer. Another trial.

Sentencing.

Twenty to twenty-five years.

Then I started school and I had to figure out my new teachers, new kids, where the bathrooms were, who to sit with on the bus, who not to sit with. I had to learn spelling and geography.

I learned to be quiet and listen, not get into trouble if at all possible so I can report to my mother every week—all good things—nothing bad. And my worlds, though a mere five miles apart, divide like the continental shift we learn about in social studies, hopefully never to meet again.

Inside and outside.

Real and unreal trade places. And then they trade back again.

Somewhere during that time Aunt Barbara becomes Matoo.

Now it's just my house, where I live; my bed, my dresser, my books, but not much from my old life, except that teddy bear.

Chapter Fourteen

Matoo doesn't make homemade anything, but you'd think from the way Margalit goes on, that there were no better chocolate chip cookies than the ones that we are having for dessert.

"Oh wow, these are so good. Can I have another one?"

Matoo looks kind of happily astounded as she passes the box across the table. "Of course, sweetie. But they're just Entenmann's."

"Oh, I don't know. But they are so good. My mother never lets me have store-bought. I mean, not that she doesn't let me, she just never buys them. These are amazing, but don't tell her I said that."

We all laugh. I guess you never know what you should be grateful for.

Matoo asks Margalit a lot of questions, which is something I never do because when you ask people questions that leaves you open to their questions about you. But I see that Matoo's technique is to ask so many questions the other person doesn't have a chance to ask you anything. Besides, she's really good at it and she remembers everything a person tells her, which is probably why she's so good at her job at the doctor's office. Everyone likes her because she remembers their names and anything they tell her.

Pretty clever, I must say.

And so far it's working. We know all about Margalit's mom and dad, what they do for a living. What kind of car they drive. Where her mom learned to cook. What kind of art the grandfather does. But I notice Margalit stays away from mentioning anything about her brother.

I understand.

I haven't said much at all until I suddenly make one of my infamously dumb statements when Margalit tells us where she lived before she moved here to Mt. Kisco. "Why have I heard of Glens Falls," I blurt out.

"Because, Ruby," Matoo says. "You used to live right near there, in Saratoga."

"Oh." And a warning light goes off in my brain. A

little late, however because Margalit is all over this one.

"You did? You lived near Glens Falls?" Margalit says. "Where? Usually when I tell people where I'm from they never heard of it. It's not that far from here really. When did you guys live there?"

Us guys didn't. Just me. And my mom.

"It was a long time ago," Matoo answers quickly. She pats both her hands on the tabletop firmly. "Well, that's it. Do you girls think you could take Loulou out for a walk before it gets too dark?"

"Oh, really? I'd love to. Can we?" Margalit jumps up.

And she forgets about Glens Falls. But I don't.

"You can just look it up."

Rebecca had all the answers. She was older than me and had been coming to the Bedford Hills children's center much longer. She had both her mother and father in jail and she knew a thing or two about jails and prisons, parol hearings, clemency boards, and, well, pretty much everything, and when I first met her, she scared me.

She was one of those tough girls. You can find them everywhere, not just in prison. I heard that there are plenty of tough girls in the middle school, ones that sneak out of the cafeteria to hang out in the bathroom, leaning on the wall or blocking your way to the stall. I heard some girls hold in their pee all day because they are too scared.

But after I got to know her, Rebecca wasn't really like that. She just wanted other kids to think she was.

"Look what up?" I asked her. We were both sitting in the seats inside the trailer. It was raining and instead of making us wait outside getting wet, like we usually have to, they let everyone pile inside the trailer and wait. There was a little corner with little-kid seats and some old books. Rebecca looked funny sitting in one of those seats. I bet I looked funny too, but she must have been at least thirteen. It was just a little while after Tevin stopped coming.

"You can look it all up," she said. "Go on the Internet. Google your mother's name. It's all public record. Court documents, newspaper articles, even transcripts of the trial if you know where to look. If you know how to search."

It seems funny now, that I never thought to do that. But at the time, it seemed perfectly normal.

"Did you do that?" I asked Rebecca.

I knew that her dad was in jail too, and she had told me that visiting her dad in prison in Ossining made Bedford Hills look like a four-star hotel.

"Sure I did," Rebecca told me. "When I was about

your age. Maybe a year older, like around twelve. I learned everything, and let me tell you, it wasn't pretty."

I can see Matoo sitting in one of the regular seats by the door, waiting our turn to show our papers, show my birth certificate, empty our pockets, sign the papers, and begin the process all over again, for the hundredth time or more. Doesn't matter if you've been here once or a million times, it's the same every time.

"What?" I asked Rebecca. "What isn't pretty?"

"Well, let's just say 'criminal justice' is an oxymoron."

I had no idea what she meant by that, but I could tell she was angry.

But I knew better than to ask. Tevin talked, but most kids didn't. And you never ask. We just don't talk like that in the children's center. Nobody says stuff like, *What did your mother do? Do you think she's guilty? Do you think she did it? Or if she did it, do you think she deserves* this?

I never thought like that. Why would I? I can't change it. Matoo says the past is the past. What good does going over it do? What good is talking about it?

"So are you glad you found out?" I asked Rebecca.

She got quiet for a bit.

She didn't answer me but I could tell whatever she found out wasn't what she thought it was going to be. Let's just say that conversation with Rebecca didn't exactly inspire me to want to run home and do the same thing.

At least not that day.

But after Margalit went home, stuffed on Entenmann's, I stay up in bed to work on my story. *Our* story. I touch my pencil to the paper at least five times before I realize I can't think of anything to write or draw. Margalit and I are both supposed to write a whole new elf chapter before camp tomorrow. But I am stuck. Is this what they call writer's block?

I can't even think of a name for my character.

I have the story notebook propped up on my knees, under the covers, all cozy for the night. My teeth are brushed. The house is quiet.

Under the green, green grass, I begin. No, not under the grass. You can't be under grass, can you?

Deep, in the dark, dark woods, Edgar the Elf makes his journey.

Edgar the Elf is stupid. I don't like that, so I erase it.

Peter the Elf.

Nah.

Josh the Elf?

Josh?

Josh Tipps. Why is that name stuck in my head?

Glens Falls? Why does that come into my head?

Saratoga. *Glens Falls.*

Glens Falls. *Saratoga.*

Josh Tipps.

I can't write. My brain won't let me think about anything else.

I look over at my computer on my desk. It's off for the night. Our computer teacher at school say it's better to just leave it on, sleeping, but Matoo can't stand leaving anything on. She unplugs the microwave when we are not using it. She even turns the router off at night, so computer waves can't penetrate our brains while we are sleeping.

But sometimes she forgets.

I slip off my bed and into my desk chair. The computer hums to life when I press the power button. If the Wi-Fi is still on, the Internet availability icon will show full access. It takes a while for everything to boot up and come flying onto my screen in bits and pieces.

The Internet is working.

I open Safari, type my mother's name and "Josh Tipps" into the search box, and while the little icon loops in circles I hold my breath.

Chapter Fifteen

While they thought I was sleeping, my mother and Nick Sands drove eighteen and a half miles away to a drugstore. There is video recording the entire two-minute-and-forty-two-seconds exchange between Nick and the boy behind the pharmacy counter, so there really wasn't much for the defense attorney to argue.

According to the *Saratoga Daily Gazette* and the district attorney of Saratoga County, Nicholas Sands, age 26, and Janis Sands, age 23, walked into the CVS on Congress Street in Glens Falls, New York. They wandered the cosmetics aisle for a while. Mrs. Sands picked up some shampoo. They then proceeded to the back of the store and approached the teenager working as a clerk in the pharmacy that night. There is a heated discussion that at some point turns aggressive on the part of Mr. Sands. In the video Mrs. Sands stands somewhat behind her husband but does not appear to be in distress, nor does she appear to be participating unwillingly.

At some point during the argument, which became increasingly more heated, Mr. Sands pulled a gun from his pocket and shot the CVS employee. He then fled the scene. Mrs. Sands is seen, in the video, climbing over the counter, where she remained on the floor beside the victim until police arrived.

There is more.

Nick Sands, who had several previous drug offenses, was charged with second-degree murder but was able to reduce his sentence, from life behind bars to eight to ten, by giving the district attorney information that led to the arrest of a well-known local drug dealer. Janis Sands was sentenced to twenty to twenty-five years in a maximum security prison.

The computer screen is the only light in my room. It is like a beacon, but it does not lead me to safety. It threatens to take it all away. I don't want to find out what I know I will find out if I keep searching. But I click link after link.

I keep searching.

There are newspaper articles. Police reports. Court

documents, all online. There are follow-up stories on everything from gun control to spousal abuse. It seems to be significant that the defendant, Janis Sands, had no knowledge of the gun prior to the incident; however, she was an accessory to an armed robbery and an accomplice to murder. The boy behind the counter died on this way to the hospital. He was seventeen years old.

His name was Joshua Alan Tipps.

Chapter Sixteen

Even after I figured out that my mother wasn't coming home with us, I still wanted to be able to at least *call* my mom whenever something bad happened to me. Not even something *that* bad, just a little bad. Like someone at school hurt my feelings or I was scared that I would never learn my times table or I had a stomachache, which usually came from one of those two other things, and I wanted to tell my mommy.

I could always tell Matoo, but it wasn't the same. For one thing, Matoo usually told me to let it go, and for another, she wasn't my mom.

"But there's the phone, right there." I stood in the kitchen in my pajamas and bare feet.

"Yes, I see the phone is right there," Matoo told

me, sitting at the breakfast table, eating her cottage cheese and berries. She took off her glasses and rubbed her eyes.

I was probably in second or third grade. No, what am I saying? It was second grade, I remember exactly, because my supposed best friend in the neighborhood, Kristin, hadn't invited me to her after school birthday party. I only found out because one girl in my class made the mistake of asking me if I was going. Of course, back then, I hadn't yet perfected the skill of how to hide important things from the outside world, and I just started crying. Right then and there, in the middle of free reading time.

Mrs. Chompsky sent me to the guidance office. The guidance lady wanted to know if my emotional state had anything to do with my "situation at home," and I had no idea what she was talking about since I didn't yet understand that I had a situation at home. I just had a home. With Matoo. And a mom at Bedford Hills Correctional Facility.

I didn't really understand yet that that wasn't normal.

I was still upset when I got back home that day, and there was the phone. And I just wanted to call my mother and tell her about it. I wanted to ask her why my only friend hadn't invited me to her birthday party and why I got sent to the office for crying in class when Lucille Ramirez does that practically every day. And Jody Bronson has not said one word out loud all year. And Donald Hancock kicks everyone under the table and everyone knows it's him. So why me?

Why? Why? Why?

There are some things only a mommy can fix.

I knew just hearing her voice would fix it. I knew she would say just the right thing and tell me I was okay, or that I was going to be okay, and I would believe her. And everything would start to be okay.

"Ruby, you know you can't call your mother," Matoo told me. "You know it doesn't work that way. She has to call us."

Us?

I didn't want her to call *us*.

I wanted her to call *me*. Me. Right now. I needed my mother, right now.

But also, I knew Matoo was right. And not only that, but my mother had to call collect, which meant someone had to be home to pick up the phone and hear the mechanical, recorded message on the other end:

"You are receiving a collect call from the Bedford Hills Correctional Facility for Women. Do you want to accept the charges?"

Matoo tells me it is very expensive, but the worst

part is how they cut you off. It doesn't matter if you are right in the middle of talking or singing or telling story. The recording comes back on, interrupts you, and warns you that you have one minute remaining. That recording is like a nightmare in my head, like a horrible bodyless, faceless voice-monster. After that minute the phone goes dead.

Mommy? Mommy? Are you there? Mommy?

"What is it you need to talk her about, Ruby? About school today? About Kristin's birthday party?" Matoo asked me.

She knew? The school *called* her?

"I took care of it, " Matoo said, before she put her glasses back on. I hoped she didn't see my mortified expression.

"You're going to the party. So get ready. You're going to meet everyone at the bowling alley in ten minutes."

Matoo was smiling. But I thought I was going to die.

I knew I couldn't call my mother but I wanted to so badly right then. I wanted to so badly that I thought maybe my wanting could be strong enough to make it happen. If only I deserved it more, never got into trouble, never did anything wrong, never cried in school—if only I did all those things, then my mother would somehow just *know* I needed her and she'd magically be calling right at this very minute.

Please, Mommy, call me.

Please call me right now.

Because if I was good enough, she'd know.

By the way, I never saw Rebecca again. Just a few weeks ago I found out that Rebecca ran away from her foster family. I overheard one of the other visitors saying she heard that Rebecca was in juvie now.

I get it.

You can run but you can't hide. And no matter what you do.

And nobody knows that better than I do now. I thought I was hiding but I wasn't. Or I was, but I can't any longer.

Josh Tipps is Margalit's brother.

I am sick.

I am so sick.

I am really so sick to my stomach and I have been all night. I didn't shut down my computer until after midnight and then I don't think I ever fell completely asleep. So I probably look pretty bad, which is good. I want Matoo to just go to work and leave me alone. When she calls up the stairs, I tell her I'm not feeling well.

There is no way I can go to camp today.

No way. I feel like I am drowning. I've never felt so alone before. I am drowning and there is no one who can save me. I just need time to think. I need time to think.

It takes a lot of convincing, but Matoo is running late and it's summer, so missing camp is not like missing school. And finally she leaves.

It's just me and Loulou now.

"Loulou, what can I do? I don't deserve this. I didn't do anything. It's so not fair. I can't tell Margalit. Ever. She can never find out."

Loulou looks at me but she doesn't have any solutions either.

I rack my brain. I consider every possibility for how to live with this terrible truth and not lose my very first, very best friend. For a crazy second, I want to call my mom—which, of course, I know I can't do— like I used to when I was little. I want her to put her arms around me and make everything all right. Or at least tell me what to do.

And then I realize my mother can't fix anything.

Because she's the one who broke it.

Chapter Seventeen

Here's another famous motto: *Where there is a will, there's a way.*

I have the will. And I sure hope I can find a way.

I don't have a plan exactly, but twenty-four hours later, and somehow I've successfully put my two worlds back where they belong—which is as far apart from each other as can be.

I just need to stay alert and keep a lid on it, which is another one of Matoo's expressions. You don't need to show everyone what you are feeling all the time, Matoo says: *Keep a lid on it.*

So I go to camp in kind of a daze, but as soon as I get there, as soon as I see Yvette and Elise and Beatrice and Margalit, and the inviting glint of the swimming pool, it's like yesterday never happened.

And the night before *that* really never happened.

I hand Margalit the story notebook, before camp even begins, and tell her how sorry I am but I just couldn't think of anything to write.

"I'm sorry," I tell her.

"That's okay," she says. "I'll do the story today and you can do the pictures, okay?"

I nod.

"So where were you yesterday?" Margalit is asking.

Yesterday is already, so effectively, gone from my memory that it takes me some time to even remember that I *wasn't* at camp.

"Oh, I had a dentist appointment." I am impressed with myself for my quick thinking. If I said I had stayed home sick, Margalit would want to know why I didn't answer the phone. She called three times.

"All day?" she asks.

"Huh?"

"I called you three times. I used Beatrice's cell phone. You couldn't have been at the dentist *all day*."

"Quiet down, you two," Yvette jumps in. She is trying to be a camp counselor today for some reason. She's decided to teach us some songs while she plays the guitar. She hands us both two paper cups.

Just as I am about to worry that this lying business isn't going to be as easy as I hoped and maybe

I should have had a better plan, Margalit drops the questioning, but adds, "It was awful here yesterday without you."

And she isn't saying it angrily. She really missed me.

I mouth: *I am sorry.*

And that's all it takes. Margalit squeezes my hand. I shut the lid and I lock it.

We are back at the clubhouse, but outside at the picnic tables between the pool and the building. Since it's during the week, there aren't many people around, but there are a few young moms with their real little babies and a few kids and a couple of teenagers like Yvette and Beatrice, which is kind of embarrassing for them, I guess, since they have to be hanging out with us.

"Okay, you guys got your part?" Yvette positions her fingers on the neck of the guitar, one at a time, and I get the impression she is just learning to play.

It takes her most of the morning to teach us the cup part. Margalit caught on really fast. After a few hundred tries, I got it too. Elise, funnily enough, got it right away. Must be all the ball-bouncing hand-eye coordination.

Yvette strums once and then starts playing and singing.

On the chorus Margalit and Elise and I join in with our cups, hitting the opening, flipping the cup over, hitting it again, and back down on its side.

We sing. Yvette taught us all the harmonies. It's actually kind of fun. Yvette's guitar playing gets better and better and our rhythm with the cups starts to happen without thinking and before you know it, we are all singing, really loud and, I think, really good. Before you know it, it's time for lunch. Margalit and I take a working lunch, writing, drawing, and eating all at the same time.

And by now, with the day more than half over, I am pretty confident that Margalit won't ever find out. I won't even say the name inside my head, ever again.

Josh Tipps.

There.

That will be the last time.

I mean, how can she ever find out? It isn't like anyone knows about my mother, so as long as I keep that a secret I am safe. Now, if I want to keep my best friend, I just need to be a little more careful, and for the first time, I am grateful that I have a different last name from my mother.

So I can be sad and thankful. Relieved and nervous. Both. It's all just a matter of keeping that lid on the pot so it doesn't boil over and mess up the stovetop.

But I can do that.

"I started a whole new story," Margalit tells me. We

are supposed to be changing for swim time, but Yvette seems ready to play her guitar again until Beatrice groans and Yvette gets her feelings hurt and while they are arguing Margalit and I go back to drawing and writing.

This pot will not boil.

"Oh, good. Can I read it now?" I ask.

"Of course," Margalit passes the notebook back to me. "I am so excited for you to read it."

Yvette is sulking and refusing to go to the pool with us. Beatrice announces free time. Elise is bouncing her ball. I open to Margalit's new pages.

This story is different. It's not about mermaids or elves or witches like our last one. Margalit is watching me read, which makes it hard, but her story is so good.

"I did something different," Margalit says. "I hope that's okay. I couldn't think of any more for the elf story."

"Yeah, me neither." I continue reading.

This story is about us. At least I think it is. It's about two girls who meet one summer at a summer camp that has only three kids and two counselors. The two girls become best friends. When I come to the end of Margalit's three pages, I look up at her.

"Marion? Is that you?" I ask her.

Margalit nods.

"And Pearl?"

I point to myself, and Margalit nods harder.

A big smile breaks out over my face. "I love it," I say.

"Whew, I'm so glad." She lets out her breath. "Okay, then, your turn. And I'll work on the illustrations."

I take the notebook and settle in. I am pretty confident now that my writer's block is cured. Margalit's story seems easier for me to follow. Real-life stuff instead of fairies and mermaids.

Write what you know. Isn't that what Ms. Genovese would say?

What comes out of my head into my fingers and down through the pen I don't think much about. I mean, I'm thinking about it, of course, but I'm not forcing it. One thing follows another easily, like a reflex.

That's another thing we learned in science class, there are voluntary and involuntary muscle movements. Like a sneeze is involuntary and the way your foot kicks up when the doctor knocks you in the knee with that little rubber hammer.

And writing a story about how your mother died when you were first born is probably, most certainly, one of those involuntary muscle action that you have no control over.

I don't even realize what I've written until I pass it back to Margalit and then I realize that in order to keep the lid on, and keep anything from spilling out, I just switched pots on the stove completely.

"Oh, Ruby," Margalit has just finished reading my chapter. "Is this true?"

I know what exactly she means.

"What do you mean?" I ask.

Ruby looks down at the notebook in her hands. "I mean, is this part true about your mother? Is that why you don't have a mother? And you live with your Matoo?"

Of course, Margalit would figure it out. She knew Matoo wasn't my mother and now she thinks she knows why.

And I did it on purpose, didn't I?

The old bait and switch.

I killed off my mother in the story because I don't want a mother, not a mother in prison. Not a mother who is ruining my life.

"Well, it was a long time ago," I say. I try not to look Margalit in the eye.

"I'm so sorry," Margalit says. She lowers her head. "I can't imagine not having a mom."

Margalit looks like she's going to cry. No one has ever cried for me. How could they? I guess. I've never told anyone about my mom, and now, the first time I have, it's a big fat lie.

No one would feel sorry for me if my mother was in prison for murder, but if my mother was dead well, that's a whole other story.

"It's okay," I say because I don't know what else to say.

"Oh, Ruby. You don't have to talk about it," Margalit says. "If you don't want to."

"I don't want to."

In my story, I wrote that my mother, or rather Pearl's mother, died in childbirth. I got that from the book *Sarah, Plain and Tall*. Luckily, I've read that book three times, so I had the details readily available.

"I'm just so sorry," Margalit is saying, wiping her eyes.

"Me too," I say.

Oh boy, if she only knew.

Chapter Eighteen

And then, just like that, another week goes uneventfully by and it's Saturday. Again.

Visiting day.

And now from the pot to the frying pan or something like that.

"Ruby, are you ready?" Matoo is standing outside my bedroom door.

I'm as far from ready as could be, but I am dressed and my bed is made and as far as I know my feet are still working. But I am standing at my bureau and looking into the mirror hanging above it, and I can't move.

Is that me in there?

The girl who does well in school. Who doesn't get into trouble. The girl that won't grow up to be like her mother.

Who am I?

Because I *am* my mother's daughter. I look just like her. When we are together, people tell us that; the other prisoners who are her friends, sometimes the guards, other visitors. And whenever somebody said that—you two look so much alike—it made me happy.

As if it was something I *could* take away with me after I left Bedford Hills. It wasn't something you could hold or touch, but it was just as real to me. I could take our connection with me wherever I went. She was my mother and I was her daughter and even if we weren't together we were bonded by this visible DNA.

The eighth characteristic of life: love.

I stand on my tiptoes and look closer. What is it people notice? Our noses? The color of my hair? My eyes? Our teeth?

And if I looked like my mother on the outside, did that mean I was going to be like her on the inside?

How can I love my mother knowing what she did? Knowing what *I* did. I lied about my mother and I said she was dead.

Is that my DNA?

Will I have to lie the rest of my life?

I force myself to smile in the mirror. I do look like my mother. The shade of our skin. And my left ear. There's a little fold at the top of my left ear, just like hers. Just like my mother's.

"Ruby, let's go." Matoo is knocking on my bedroom door again.

"Okay," I answer.

There's a huge, long line when we get to Bedford Hills. It's going to take forever to get inside. But today I don't care.

I'm in no hurry.

Today, I am not looking forward to getting inside. I don't know what I am going to say.

"Ruby, what's with you today? You're not yourself." Matoo parks the car in the lot. I wonder how I never noticed before how horrible and ugly this place is.

Suddenly it looks like a prison in a scary movie. The old crumbling brick buildings that look deserted or haunted or both. The indescribably tall chain link fence with the razor wire running over the top, hundreds of blades, and for the first time I let myself know why it is there.

To keep the bad guys in.

So that if someone tried to escape, if they tried to climb over that fence, forcing their toes into the space between the links, gripping with their fingers, they would only be cut to shreds when they tried to make their way over the top to the other side. I have seen that fence a million times and now I know.

"I'm fine," I tell Matoo.

We take our place in line and wait forty-five minutes before we are at the door to the trailer where we will be processed. When we finally get inside, the air conditioning is blasting. There will be no air conditioning when we get to the visiting room. It's been broken for weeks and no one can say when it will be fixed. And there is no air conditioning at all in the housing units.

Because this is a prison. It's not supposed to be comfortable.

When we get into security Matoo takes out a quarter and opens a locker. She stuffs her pocketbook inside and looks at me. When I was little I used to beg her to let me put the quarter in, like it was a game at a carnival.

But it is not a carnival. There is no fairy tale that ends like this.

"Do you have anything to put in?" Matoo asks me.

I dig into my pocket and lift out my open palm. I have some change, a dime, two nickels, and five pennies. I think they have been in these shorts from the day Margalit and I were diving for coins in the pool.

I feel a knot growing in my stomach. How many things have I chosen not to see?

So many.

Like every winter my middle school does a fund-raiser or toy drive or a mitten-and-glove collection for poor people. Last Christmas there were a bunch of big cardboard boxes set up in the lobby with a tall color sign. The eighth graders were collecting "new in the package" toys for the "women of Bedford."

I walked right by it and didn't think about it at all.

I didn't want to think about it.

I might have glanced once or twice at the growing piles of toys, games, and stuffed animals. But it wasn't until I recognized the toy my mother "gave" me for Christmas did I put it together. Some kid at my school donated that gift and now here it was in my hands.

But so what?

I put it out of my head.

It was way too babyish a gift, but I never let on. I didn't want to hurt my mother's feelings. I hugged the toy—I don't even remember what it was—and pretended that I loved it. And I did love it. Because my mother had picked it out for me.

But now the CO is asking me to walk through the metal detector with my arms out to the side, and I am thinking that the gift my mother gave me for Christmas last year was a gift someone else got for their birthday they didn't even want enough to open.

"Step up here, please," the CO says. She is wearing rubber gloves.

I step up and she runs the wand all around my body. When I was little I thought that the rays coming out of it could read my mind. I used to try and make my mind blank so they wouldn't know what I was thinking. So they wouldn't know that I was scared, and excited, angry, and sad, and nervous, and happy to be finally getting to see my mother again.

Now Matoo and I pass through the bars. The thick black bars just like in cartoons where the man in jail is resting his hands and trying to press his face out. Because this is a prison.

"Right hand, please."

We are at the Plexiglas window with only a small opening where I am supposed to reach in with the top of my hand facing up. The officer behind the glass stamps my hand with an invisible stamp. Today it is the right hand. Yesterday must have been left. I am not sure why they switch it every day, but I am sure it has something to do with preventing the prisoners from getting out. Or the wrong people from coming in.

Now we have to walk outside again.

There is a whole line of us, staggered, depending on how long you took to pass through security. The man behind the Plexiglas pushes a button and those black metal bars slide open. We are walking from one building into the prison itself. I can see more razor wire right over my head. It is so close I can see the sun glinting off its edges.

Matoo puts her arm around me for a short squeeze. She can tell something is wrong but we keep walking.

Here there is a little machine that you have to put your hand under and suddenly, there it is, the glowing stamp they just put on your skin. I used to think that was so cool, so magical.

Not anymore.

My heart is racing. I know the next stop is for our table assignment and, wouldn't you know it, it's Officer Rubins.

"Good morning, ladies," he says.

I look down at the floor.

"Good morning," Matoo answers.

I don't say anything which is not like me, but this isn't a day care center. Nobody cares.

"Table sixteen," Officer Rubins says. He checks us off. Now it's up to him when he decides to call the housing unit and let them know that prisoner 556731 has visitors.

That is the number my mother has to recite when they do a count. Twice a day, every day, or more if they need to. Not Janis Danes, her maiden name. Not even Janis Sands, her married name. But prisoner 556731.

Matoo had explained to me that the prison count was like Buddy count on a field trip. And I used to believe that. It reminded me of being at the Bronx Zoo when Mrs. Clark blew her whistle and shouted, *Buddy count!* We had to stop whatever we were doing, find our assigned buddy, and hold our clasped hands up in the air. We couldn't lower our arms until Mrs. Clark had counted each and every one of us.

I loved Mrs. Clark. She was one of my favorite teachers. You could just tell she cared so much about us. She wanted to make sure we were all safe and that she hadn't lost anyone in the zoo.

"This is a big, huge park," she told us. "I want us to have fun, but I don't want anyone to wander away from the group and be scared."

Matoo and I sit down at our table and wait.

My mother let me get lost.

And now I have to find myself.

Chapter Nineteen

For the longest time I thought that my mother got put in prison because she got in trouble. "Trouble" the way kids use it.

Like: *Don't do that—you'll get in trouble.*

Or worse: *Better not do that you'll get in big trouble.*

So for a long time, I was terrified of getting in trouble. Of being bad. And for some reason, I felt like I was always just a hair away from doing something wrong. And getting in trouble.

But sometimes trouble just sneaks up and smacks you in the back of the head.

"Ow." I turned around.

I watched a pencil roll across my desk and hit the floor. Someone had thrown a pencil at me. It was Trevor, I was sure.

Trevor was a bully. He bothered kids for no reason. He didn't seem to care who he hurt and he never got caught. I suspect that he was aiming for the boy in front of me but I got hit.

I was only in third grade at the time, old enough to know better, but I leaned over and picked up the pencil. I even looked up at the front of the room and waited until I saw our Spanish teacher writing on the board. And then I threw the pencil back at him. It whirled through the air, tip over eraser, in a nice easy glide. I hadn't meant to, but it was aimed right at Trevor's face. He wasn't expecting it, so he wasn't looking and it hit him—just my luck—point forward, right in his cheek.

It stuck there for what felt like ten seconds, was probably just a split second, but long enough to leave a deep black imprint, and then fell.

Trevor jumped up.

"Oh, God. I've been poisoned," he shouted. "Ruby Danes stabbed me with a pencil. Look." He couldn't have seen it himself but he pointed right to the mark on his face. Of course, everybody looked. Including Señora Bavido.

Trevor got sent to the nurse and I got in-school detention for two days. No recess. After lunch I had to report to my classroom and sit at my desk while everyone else was outside playing.

I could look right out the window. There was Kristin running around with a bunch of girls. I wasn't really friends with them, but I had known them for two whole years. I knew they were playing TV tag, a game that if you can shout out the name of a TV show and squat down before you get tagged you are safe. I didn't have a best friend, but if I was out there, I probably would have been playing TV tag too.

When Kristin ran right by the big glass window I lifted my hand to wave.

I don't even think Kristin saw me.

Matoo knew I had gotten detention. She had to sign a piece of paper saying she knew.

"Don't worry about it, Ruby," she told me that morning. "It wasn't your fault. Just be more careful next time. Don't throw pencils even if someone threw one at you first. You don't want to get into trouble."

No, of course not. I didn't try to get into trouble.

I didn't even try to hit Trevor. I could throw that same pencil a hundred times and not hit him like that ever again. I stand at the plate for Wiffle ball every year in gym class and I've never the ball once. Hitting Trevor right in the cheek with that skinny pencil was the definition of an accident and yet there I was. In detention.

I looked outside again at the world that was kept

from me and then it occurred to me. Was I being kept from the world?

Had I been so bad that everyone out there was in danger of being stabbed in the face by a crazy pencil-wielding eight-year-old?

I raised my hand.

"There's no talking in detention," the detention teacher said. "But what is it?"

"Why am I here?" I asked her.

"You know exactly why you are here." The teacher quickly shuffled through some papers on the desk that wasn't hers, but she was using for this period, to guard me and the only other kid in the room, Carlos, who didn't do his homework for a whole week and had no excuse.

"I mean, *why* why? What good will it do?"

"You will learn a lesson," she said. She stopped looking for whatever she was looking for. "You are being punished. Kids today think there are no repercussions. Do you know that means?"

I nodded. I did.

"Consequences," Carlos shouted from the back of the room. He was supposed to be doing his homework while he was here, so *his* detention made a little more sense to me.

"Exactly," the teacher said.

"But I didn't do anything on purpose."

"There are consequences for accidents, too. Young people need to learn to be responsible for their actions."

I thought about that. It didn't make sense. I knew I could have chosen not to throw the pencil but I still didn't see why sitting here instead of playing outside was teaching me a lesson. It was just making me sad and mad and lonely.

Now I just really hated Trevor Sullivan for being a bully and for never getting caught and for getting me trouble because of his big mouth.

"Yeah, Ruby. No one made you throw that pencil," Carlos said. I think he liked talking more than doing his math homework. He didn't want the conversation to end.

"Is that what happened?" the teacher asked.

"Yeah," I said. "But the other kid threw it at me first. I've never thrown a pencil before."

"And I bet you'll never do it again. Huh, Ruby?" Carlos added.

That was true.

"Maybe that's the best we can do," the teacher said.

"So that's my lesson?" I asked the teacher but I knew the answer. I was being punished and Trevor wasn't, and that was just the way it was. So sure the world was a safer place but not for me.

At the end of the period, Carlos bolted out the door. I just sat there.

"I know it seems unfair." The teacher came over and stood by my desk.

If she was now going to tell me that life's unfair, I thought I was going to throw a pencil at *her*.

"And in many ways it is, Ruby. I know."

It is?

"And for what it's worth, I'm sorry you didn't get to play outside today. But I have to say, I did enjoy talking with you. Maybe you'll get detention again and we'll get to spend more time together."

I knew she was joking.

She meant to be nice, but I didn't think it was funny at all.

Chapter Twenty

Right now, while Matoo and I are waiting at table sixteen, I can see there are three little kids in the children's center: two little girls, and a boy who looks like he's about five years old. They are coloring and playing games because they don't understand.

Maybe one of them will try and ask the corrections officer to let her take her mother home. Maybe that little girl thinks today is soon enough. Today she's waited for so long, and she's been so good, done everything everyone told her. So why isn't her mother coming home with her?

To cook her dinner. To tuck her into bed. To tell her she's good and pretty and loved. Help her with her homework. And tell her that everything's going to be okay.

Life is unfair. Everybody knows that. Teachers and parents say it all the time. But if everyone knows it, why do they let it happen?

Why doesn't somebody do something about it?

Life wouldn't be so unfair if people did something about it.

I know that what my mother did was a lot worse than throwing a pencil. She left her daughter alone in an apartment and went with her husband to hold up a store, because he asked her to, and someone who didn't deserve to, someone who was totally innocent, lost their life.

No, some*one* didn't lose their life that day.

Two people did.

Josh Tipps. And me. I lost the life I was supposed to have that day too.

Maybe if she hadn't gone, Nick wouldn't have gone. Maybe if she had just been a little stronger and said, *No, this isn't right*, he wouldn't have done it. At least not that night, not the night that Margalit's brother, Josh, was working behind the counter.

Maybe if my mother had loved me more than she wanted Nick to love her, none of this would have happened at all. If my mother loved me at all, she wouldn't have let this happen.

I hate her now for not loving me enough. I hate

myself for not being lovable enough.

I hear that sound, the door cranking open. And there she is, walking in through the door behind the big desk where Officer Rubins is sitting, the big desk with the paper chimney.

I am angry. I am so angry. It's not going to work.

My mother ruined my life and it's only going to get worse. The first best friend I've ever had is going to find out who I really am. She's going to find out what my mother did. Sooner or later she's bound to find out.

And then she'll hate me forever and I didn't even do anything.

And even if Margalit never finds out, *I'll* know. I'll know that I'm lying to my best friend every day.

My mother doesn't see us right away. She walks into the visitors' room and I watch her looking all around. She is, of course, in green, all green. Visitors are not allowed to wear green, but that's not a problem for me. I've made sure I don't own one green thing. Not a shirt, or a sweater, a sweatshirt, or pants. Not even green socks.

My mother's hair is pulled back in a simple ponytail. She looks young, I think. Younger than other moms I've seen at school. I've only ever seen her this way. Her hair up or her hair down. Sometimes she wears a little makeup. Sometimes none at all. But always in green. She doesn't seem to get older. But I have.

She hasn't seen us yet, because usually I call out her name and start waving from my seat. Today I can't. My inside and my outside are colliding. Everything is about to spill over the top, making a mess on the stovetop.

And I make a little sound, that same little gasp that came out of Larissa's mouth when she saw her mom come into the room. It comes from a place that is so deep, so old, and so wounded. It just escapes from your heart without your consent. Like finding a piece of your own body that was broken off and now, there you see it. It's so close. There it is.

My mom sees us.

I can tell by the look on her face, even from this far across the whole room: recognition. She knows me.

I am her daughter.

And she is my mother.

And Rebecca? Where is she now? She didn't keep anything inside and look where that got her. Look how it hurt her. I imagine her on the streets somewhere, all alone. Just standing there, waiting. Except no one knows where she, is so she's waiting for nothing.

My mother is walking this way. She has a big smile on her face.

And Tevin?

I do miss Tevin. He was always so hopeful. It was infectious, like he would never give up and he never had to. Not in my mind, where he lives now. In my mind, he will always believe in soon.

My mother must not see the hard, steely expression on my face because she bends down and hugs me just like it's any other regular visiting day. Just like nothing has changed. Because for her, nothing has. But for me, everything has changed.

"Oh, my sweetie. My sweetheart. My Ruby heart," my mother says.

I try and tell my outside to stiffen up and protect me, but my inside doesn't listen and when my mother's arms are all the way around me, my inside breaks into a million little pieces.

"What's wrong, baby?" my mother is saying. She doesn't let go. She holds me tighter. "What is it? You can tell me. Tell me, sweetheart. Tell me what's wrong."

"I'm so mad at you," I yell. I think I yell. It sounds like a yell inside my head. I say it again and I wait for the whole world to fall apart but instead I feel my mother's strong arms around my shoulders, pressing my whole body into hers. Her voice is my mother's voice, will always be my mother's voice. Her skin is her skin, is her skin is her hair, is my skin and my hair, and her eyes and her hands, and my heart and her heart.

And now all I can do is cry.

They make me leave the visitors' room. They don't allow outbursts of excessive emotion. I guess it's like a yawn. It can trigger everyone else to start yawning. Or sobbing, as the case may be. I make a beeline for the bathrooms just past the first set of doors.

I'm outside now. I can't go back in without going through all those procedures.

And then, Matoo is sitting in the bathroom with me.

Just thinking about how awful my mother feels right now, because of me, makes me sick to my stomach. The scene I made, she was powerless to prevent, powerless to help, powerless to even stay and wait for me to calm down. They will take her away now. They will put hours, days, weeks of metal bars between us, all because I couldn't control myself.

I *can't* control myself.

"I'm going to be sick, Matoo," I say.

"It's okay. Here." She walks me into the stall, pushing open the door with one hand and holding back my hair with the other.

I puke. I mean I really puke.

"It's okay," Matoo says when I am finished. "Rinse up. Splash some water on your face." She walks me over to the sinks.

My mother is gone.

She's gone. There nothing and no power on earth or in heaven that's going let me see my mother again today. I sent her away. I did that. I hurt my mother. I know she's a mess now, wondering what's wrong with me and not being able to do anything about it. She'll want to call, but she can't just use the phone whenever she wants to.

I know she'll want to.

I start sobbing all over again and now I feel like I'm going to throw up a second time. I am thinking about my mother and Margalit, and Josh Tipps. And Margalit's mother, who will hate me forever. How could she not?

She should.

I hate myself.

And if, by some miracle, she didn't hate me, she'd never be able to look at me the same.

It's all ruined. I've lost my best friend and I've lost my mother.

"Breathe," Matoo says. "Try and calm down. Then tell me what's going on."

I don't throw up again, but I feel my legs getting

weaker. My knees give out and my whole body slides down along the wall until I am sitting on the floor.

I can see it in Matoo's face: *Oh, that dirty floor. That dirty wall.*

Ruby, she wants to say, *what's the matter with you? It's filthy in here. Straighten yourself up. Stand up. Pull yourself together.*

Get over it. Put it lid on it.

But she doesn't.

I watch as Matoo slithers down, her back against the wall, until she slides right next to me. She doesn't let her bottom touch, but instead she kind of balances on the heels of her shoes.

"Tell me, Ruby. What's going on?"

Chapter Twenty-One

Once upon a time, a long time ago, before I was born, there were two sisters who lived in an apartment alone with their mother; just three weeks earlier their dad had run off with another woman. So now it was just the three of them, and because the mom started spending a lot of time in bed, the older sister had to do a lot, like making meals and making beds and making sure the two sisters got to school on time.

And the mother kept sleeping a lot.

And then one morning the mother didn't wake up forever.

Since their dad was nowhere to be found and their mom was now gone, the two sisters went to live with strangers but at least they got to stay together. Things in that house of strangers were not always nice. But still, the older sister tried to keep things as normal as she could, as tight as she could, as controlled as she could. She vowed she would always take care of her little sister.

But the world around them was out of control.

And then the two sisters grew up. One stayed as close to the rules and limits as she could, pushing only the buttons she knew would work. The other sister, the younger one, kept running around, edging close to the limits, peeking over the top, pushing any button she could, as if she was trying to find the one that would wake up their mother that morning and make everything safe again.

"That was my mother?" I ask Matoo. "The younger sister?"

"Yes, sweetheart. That was your mother." Matoo is still crouching with me on the bathroom floor. A few people have come and gone. They take one look at us, do their business, wash their hands and leave. No one seems to think it's strange.

Here, nothing is strange. No one is judged because everyone has been judged already.

"And then after your real father—may God rest his soul."

"My real father is dead?"

"I have no idea, and neither does your mother. I'm just saying that out of disrespect."

"Oh."

Matoo went on. "Anyway, after your biological father left, and your mother met Nick, well, we all thought things were going to be better for her. For both of you. Well, *I* never thought that. Your mother did. She was looking for a dream, Ruby, you have to understand. Nick was like her mother and father all rolled into one. He built things and planted things and took care of the house. And he brought her cups of tea with honey and cream. No one ever did anything like that for her before. She was afraid to lose him."

I look at Matoo. I know no one ever did anything like that for her, either.

"So I understand why she went with him that night," Matoo said.

"But she left me," I say.

"I know, Ruby. She made a terrible mistake. I don't think your mother ever understood how important she was to you. She didn't think she was important to anyone. She felt worthless, and so to her, leaving you alone for what she thought would be a few minutes didn't seem that important. I know it doesn't make sense."

It did. I know what it's like to think you are not important, not special. To think that what you do doesn't matter or make a difference.

"But Nick was dangerous," I prompted her.

"He was. And your mother knew it, right from the start. But it was like he was offering a drink of water and she was so terribly thirsty. She had been walking in the desert all her life."

"But the water was poison."

"It was."

We are both quiet for a while. I never really studied the underside of a row of industrial sinks before. It's not real pretty.

"I think we should go, Matoo," I say.

"Are you ready?"

"Just one more thing."

"Of course."

"The boy that died that night. Josh. Josh Tipps," I begin.

"Yes?"

"His family would hate my mother, wouldn't they? They wouldn't care about that story, about being thirsty or living with strangers or your mother dying, would they? They would just hate us."

Matoo stands up. I can tell her legs are stiff and aching. She's always complaining about her bones, her back and the pain that runs down her arm. But I think there are other aches that she doesn't ever talk about that are her real pain.

"I don't know, they might. They might not. But what made you think about them? How do you even know that name?"

I'm staying on the floor. It seems safer down here. I feel smaller. I wish I were little again, when I didn't know any of this.

I answer her. "I've heard you say that name and then I found it on the Internet. I read about the whole thing. About the boy who got shot. About the trial. About everything. It's so awful, Matoo. My mother is responsible for Margalit's brother dying, being killed."

Before I can feel sick again, Matoo is right next to me again. She groans a little but she crouches back down.

"Ruby, what are you talking about?" Matoo is saying. "What does any of this have to do with Margalit? Josh Tipps's parents don't even live around here. They live in Virginia. Well, the father does. The mother is in Utah or something like that."

There is a kind of buzzing in my ear and the tip of my nose. "What?"

"We've been in touch with them, Ruby. Your mother writes them letters all the time. We just didn't think you'd want to hear about that. Not yet. Josh's father even came to visit your mother once."

"Josh Tipps is not Margalit's brother?" I ask.

The buzzing is getting louder and moving into my whole face. My heart is thumping out of my control. My whole face is numb.

"Margalit's brother? No, why? Is her last name Tipps?"

"Yes," I say.

"And she has a brother who was killed?"

Yes, I mean. I don't know. He died somehow. I think . . . so I just thought . . ."

Now Matoo starts crying a little too. "You thought the Josh Tipps from that night was Margalit's brother who died?"

I nod.

"Oh, baby girl. No wonder you've been so upset. No, Ruby. You don't have to worry about that. We've got enough to worry about."

I am still a little confused. "Are you sure?"

"What, sweetie?

"Are you sure there's another Josh Tipps?"

"Yes, Ruby. I'm positive. I saw the Tippses at the trial. Every day for months, and I've met Margalit's parents. They are not the same people. It's just one of those crazy things. It's just a name."

"It's just a name," I repeat.

So my life is not ruined. Not completely. Not yet. Not at all.

"Let's go home now, okay? Maybe your mother will be able to call and we can straighten this all out."

"Okay."

I get up first, so I can help Matoo. My legs are pretty stiff now too. I rub my bottom. It's so cold from the tile floor, but I feel better than I've felt in a lot of days. Like a thousand pounds have been taken off my chest, my back, my shoulders, and my head, which is pretty good considering there's another thousand still there, but it's better than it was before.

Chapter Twenty-Two

We are eating dinner and waiting to see if my mother calls. Loulou is sitting under the table in case one of us drops something. She's sitting right under *my* feet, of course. I poke around at my Chinese food.

"I'm sure she'll call as soon as she can," Matoo is saying.

"Is your cell phone charged?"

"It is, but she'll call the landline, you know that."

Matoo gets up and starts cleaning. She won't leave the leftovers in those cardboard boxes. She says they leak and make a mess in the refrigerator. She puts everything into fresh, clean containers and lines them up on the middle shelf.

I drop a little piece of roast pork lo mein for Loulou and I wait.

I remember when I used to think that phones only worked in one direction because we never called my mother. We always waited for her to call us and for the longest time I didn't understand that you could make an outgoing call, until kids started getting their own iPhones. And even then, I thought it must be some new cellular technology.

Wait, what? You are allowed to call someone first?

"Maybe she's mad at me," I say.

"Oh, goodness. Your mother would never be mad at you."

How many times we've sat at this kitchen table and waited. My mother tries to call at the same time every week, but there are exceptions. There are rules and circumstances that come before everything. There might be a lockdown. Or a change in mealtime for her unit. She is not allowed to call during work hours, or cleaning detail, or mealtime, or counts, or lockdowns, or after or before hours. Someone else makes every decision for her. Every choice about her life is made by someone else. Some*thing* else.

I once heard my mother telling Matoo she was afraid she was forgetting how to be a grown-up.

"Let's have some ice cream while we wait," Matoo says. She's put away all the Chinese food, done the dishes, and wiped the drips of duck sauce that, of course, I spilled.

"Do we have whipped cream?"

"We sure do."

So Matoo and I have ice-cream sundaes and the sun drops lower and lower in the sky outside our window. An orange light spreads across the whole room. We should turn on the lights but neither one of us moves from the table. We are both eating as slowly as we can.

I love it best when the ice cream melts and mixes with the whipped cream and it's like scooping up thick, sweet ice-cream soup into my spoon. I don't want to enjoy it, but I do, and I bet Margalit would love this dessert. I bet she would love the Cool Whip that we always keep in the freezer. Sometimes I sneak and just take a scoop right out of the tub.

Things are going to be all right.

And now I know that if I am going to keep Margalit as my friend, my best friend, I think I need to tell her the truth.

"Matoo, there's something I need to do," I say. "Can I take Loulou for a walk?"

"Right now?" she asks me.

"I think so."

"What if your mother calls?"

"Tell her the truth. Tell her I had to go see my friend," I say. "Do you think she'll understand?"

"I know she will," Matoo says. "Here. Take a flashlight with you."

I nod. Even though Matoo doesn't like me walking around after dark, she lets me.

Loulou is stopping at every fence post to either sniff, or sniff, squat down, and pee on top of whatever it is she is smelling. I thought only boy dogs did that. But I let her take as much time as she likes.

I like the condo neighborhood at night like this. No one is around, just a few other people walking their dogs. A couple of people, a man and a woman are all dressed up coming down their stairs to their car. I guess they are going out for a Saturday-night party or something. But mostly it's empty and quiet. I especially love walking by the pool at night. The water is perfectly still, like a mirror. There is only one little yellow light on by the clubhouse that lights up just that one section of concrete and a patch of green grass.

I have one long block to figure out what I am going to tell Margalit. I know I want to do it now. Before camp Monday. Before I chicken out.

What am I going to tell her?

I know what I *want* to tell her. I want Margalit to

know that I love my mother, that my mother is not dead like Caleb's mother in *Sarah, Plain and Tall*, and that my mother is in prison.

That's where I was today, Margalit. Visiting my mother in prison. And that's where I'll be every Saturday unless we have something more important to do. If, that is, you still want to be my friend, and we have something more important or fun to do.

I am imagining the whole conversation in my head and so far it's going pretty well.

Or maybe I'm actually talking out loud.

"Excuse me? Are you saying something to me?" It's Mrs. Hochreiter, walking her dog, Ringo.

I look up.

"Oh, no. Sorry." I say. "Just talking to myself."

Loulou and Mrs. Hochreiter's golden retriever are sniffing each's bottoms and Loulou ends up walking right under Ringo's whole body so that our leashes get all tangled.

"No worries," Mrs. Hochreiter says. She drops her end of the leash and lets Ringo untangle himself. "I talk to myself all the time."

When Mrs. Hochreiter and Ringo move past I see Margalit. She is heading right toward me.

"Ruby," she calls out. "I was just going to your house. I mean, I just called your house and your mom said you were . . . I mean your Matoo . . . I mean, I was hoping . . . Oh, Loulou, oh hi, Loulou!"

By the time she is done talking we are standing right next to each other. Loulou is wagging her tail like crazy, trying not to jump up onto Margalit because she knows she's not supposed to jump on people.

"It's okay," I say. "I was just coming to you."

"You were?"

There is a little worn dirt path that winds through the woods, around all the condo units, the pool, the clubhouse, and all the parking lots. Without saying anything, we start walking that way, the three of us. Then, when we get near the woods that separates the whole condo unit from the road, the mosquitoes join us.

Margalit is swatting her hand around her head like crazy. "This one bug," she says. "It's been flying around my ear the whole time. Why won't it go away?"

I've got one by me, too. A buzzing unseen insect circling me no matter how far or how fast we walk.

"Oh, I know." I am holding Loulou's leash in one hand and waving my hand from my face to the back of my neck.

"Don't you ever wonder how this tiny bug can wander so far away from home?" Margalit is asking, and swatting.

"What do you mean?"

"I mean, for us to walk around this path is no big deal but for this tiny bug it's the equivalent of like hundreds of miles, isn't it?" She bats at the air next to her ear. "So this bug stays flying around your head, it won't go away but we are still walking, so it's moving farther and farther from its home. Doesn't its family wonder where it is? How will it find its way back?"

I never thought of that. What a dumb little bug. "I don't know. Do bugs have homes?"

Margalit looks at me. "I think so. They're supposed to. I mean, if they are alive, then they were born, they must have a family of two or three hundred brothers and sisters, and a father and a mother and . . ." She finally stops talking.

I felt like I am standing at the end of the diving board when you are so scared but if there's one second when the thought enters your head to jump, you jump. I start, "Margalit, my mother's not dead. I got that from a book."

"*Sarah, Plain and Tall?*"

"You know it?"

Margalit nods. "Yeah, I thought it sounded familiar. Especially when you used the name Caleb for the pet dog. That was kind of a dead giveaway."

"But you didn't say anything."

"Well, I figured there was something you'd tell me when you felt like it," Margalit said.

"Yeah, something like that."

Loulou stops to sniff at a tuft of tall grass that looks exactly like the tuft of tall grass we just passed a few seconds ago but apparently to Loulou it's something completely new and exciting. Her nostrils flare open at the sides and she sucks in the air.

"My mother's in prison." I say it.

Loulou looks up to the sound of my voice, like maybe my tone startled her, but then she just continues to waddle ahead. Margalit and I fall into step with her.

"Oh," Margalit says.

She looks like she doesn't know what to say or think or feel. And I sure can't blame her for that.

"I've never told anyone that before. You are the first one," I say.

"I'm glad you told me," Margalit says.

We keep walking, which is good because we both have to look straight ahead in the direction we are going. And you should always look down, in case some other dog wasn't as considerate as Loulou, to go in the bushes.

"So Matoo is not your mother?"

"No," I tell her. "She's my aunt. She's my mother's

sister. Barbara. Her real name is Barbara, but she's like—"

"Like your Mom, too?"

"Yeah, exactly," I say.

"Matoo. I like that," Margalit says.

"So you're not mad at me?" I ask, keeping my gaze focused on the ground.

"Of course not," Margalit says. But I am not that convinced.

"I didn't mean to lie to you. I just never wanted anyone to know."

I feel Margalit's fingers reaching for my hand. When she has it, she squeezes it. "I get that, but I'm not anyone," she says. "I'm your best friend."

I always knew I wanted a best friend, but I never knew a best friend would want me.

"And I am yours," I say.

"To be continued."

"To be continued."

We walk the path, holding hands, Loulou leading the way.

Chapter Twenty-Three

It's nearly the end of August, and I can already see summer getting ready to leave, in the way the morning light comes a little later. I can hear it in the dryness of the leaves blowing outside my screen window in the morning.

My last visit with my mom feels like it was a month ago instead of a week, which is what it was. The beginning of summer feels like a life time ago. And best of all, it feels like me and Margalit have been friends forever. Best friends.

School starts in a mere two weeks. Now every day really counts.

Slowly, Margalit started telling me little bits about her brother. She has a sad story too. Her brother died of a blood cancer three years before Margalit was born.

She never knew him, but sometimes, when she is telling the story, she just leaves that part out. Sometimes, she told me quietly, sometimes she's more sad that she didn't know her brother than that he died. She feels left out of the mourning and the memories her parents share. She feels jealous, even angry, and then she feels guilty for feeling that way.

This does not surprise me. And it does not scare me away. So far, things I've told Margalit haven't scared her off either.

If I had done the math I might have figured out earlier that Margalit's brother could not have been the same Josh Tipps, but I think when you are trying so hard to hide your own truth, it's hard to see anyone else's.

Margalit and I still go to camp every day, but things are winding down there, too. Beatrice and Yvette pretty much gave up on being real camp counselors and mostly we all just hang out at the pool, all five of us, just like a group of friends.

"Hey, whatever happened to that little book of yours?" Beatrice asks.

"We still have it," Margalit answers quickly.

I have it, but we haven't been writing together for a while.

"*To be Continued*. That was a cool title," Yvette says.

Elise started her own little book too, which was mostly pictures of mermaids and elves. At lunch she forced us all to listen and look at her illustrations.

They were cute, even if she was nothing but a big copycat.

But what Margalit didn't tell anyone was that all week the book has been at my house because I started another story and this one was all mine. I started a story about a girl named Trudy whose mother was in prison. And, whoosh, everything came out. I wrote about how it felt not live with your mother, not to be able to see or talk to her when you wanted, and not to be able to tell anyone where she was.

And about how angry it made me—I mean, Trudy. And how sad it made her. Trudy got to ask all the questions I had never felt like I could ask. And she could say all the things I thought I should never say. Trudy could be bad and lie about things. She could get in trouble. She could get angry and she could cry whenever she felt like it.

Sometimes I read my story to Margalit over the phone before I go to sleep.

It was Margalit's idea that I show it to my mother. Then the more I thought about that, the more I want to do it.

"But first we need a title," Margalit says.

"I don't need a title."

"Every good story needs a title."

"What I really need is a cell phone," I say. "So we can text each other if we aren't in any of the same classes this year."

"Don't change the subject," Margalit tells me over the phone.

"But we're going to be in middle school. Everyone has a cell phone," I say.

I am under my covers, with my notebook. I just finished reading my last chapter out loud to Margalit. The one where the bully stabs Trudy with a pencil in the classroom and she gets in trouble for it but she gets to make a big, long speech at the end and everyone cheers. So it's worth it. Margalit liked that chapter.

"Title," Margalit insists.

"I don't know. I won't be able to bring this to my mom anyway. They don't allow you to bring any books. There's inside rules and there's outside rules."

"Oh, that's it," Margalit says suddenly.

"That's what?"

"The title for your book. *Ruby on the Outside*."

"You mean Trudy."

"Yeah, *Trudy on the Outside*."

I like it.

Chapter Twenty-Four

At first, Margalit kept wanting to know why I couldn't just bring the story with me on my visit, and that is the stuff that's hard to explain. And even as I am saying some things I wonder if it's too much.

"Because they don't want people smuggling things inside."

"In a book?"

"Well, yeah, like under the pages glued together."

I could tell Margalit didn't understand, and to tell the truth, neither do I. But I know people have tried to put drugs in there. I don't really get it, but some drugs I guess can be put into the glue and licked or eaten.

It's too gross to even think about, but that's one of the reasons you can't bring books or photo albums, and glitter is a big no-no.

"It's better if you just mail things," I tell her.

"So mail it," Margalit says.

Still, everything will be taken apart, inspected, and dissected, and that takes forever. All you can do is hope they get to it, sooner rather than later. The COs will go through every box. They will read all our letters and they record our phone calls. People mail food all the time, and half the time it goes bad before it reaches the person it was meant for.

They will read my story, my very private story. But Margalit is right, it's the only way.

So Matoo mails my notebook and maybe it will get to my mother before our next visit. Maybe it won't.

It is embarrassing to tell Margalit stuff like this. Actually, most everything is hard to talk about, and thankfully, even though she asks about a lot of things, Margalit still hasn't asked that one question.

It's like she just knows not to, like Rebecca or Larissa or Tevin would never ask.

You just don't talk about things like that.

Margalit hasn't asked what my mother did to get herself locked in prison for twenty to twenty-five years without parole. I'm glad she never asks, because there are some questions that have no answers.

Life is unfair like that.

"Did your mom get your package?" Margalit asks

me Friday afternoon. She calls me as soon as I get in the door from camp. I have to run into the kitchen to answer it before the machine picks up. She calls me even though we just saw each other a few minutes ago.

"I don't know," I tell her. "I won't know till tomorrow."

I really need my own phone.

"Good luck," Margalit says.

This time when my mom walks into the visitors' room she doesn't come over and throw her arms around me like she usually does. This time she waits for me. My mom sits down at the table.

"I'm going to get some coffee," Matoo says. She pushes her chair back and stands.

I can tell from the way she looks at my mother that they've discussed this already on the phone. Matoo is going to give us some privacy. There is no privacy in prison, so this is as close as we can get.

Actually, I'm nervous when Matoo leaves.

My mother starts. "I got your story, Ruby. You are a wonderful writer. You're so talented. I loved Trudy. She's a great character. She's got a lot of courage, like you, Ruby."

I know a mother is supposed to say that, but still, it feels good.

"So do you want me to talk about it?" my mother asks me.

I do, of course I do. But I can already feel our time disappearing, being taken from me. There's big clock above the CO's tall desk and it's moving in fast motion. I can hear the ticking of the second hand from here.

"Sure," I say.

I hear my mother taking a deep breath, but I still haven't lifted my eyes to see hers.

"You want to know what really happened? That night?"

I am silent. I can't say either way, if I want to know more or I don't. I really just want to be a kid. I don't want to have to hear this, but I don't want *not* to. I bury my face in my arms, crossed on the table, and all I have now is her voice.

Like all she had was my voice, when I wrote that story, and then she read it.

"Have I ever really said I'm sorry, Ruby?" my mother starts. "Have I?"

I keep my head hidden and she goes on, "I'm so sorry, Ruby. I'm sorry that my mistakes have affected your whole life and and every aspect of it. That is something I have to live with. And for as long as you need to talk about it, or cry, or be angry, or write about it, I will listen to you."

In my story, Trudy was so angry in ways I didn't even know I felt until I wrote them down. Now my mother knows too. But she keeps talking, softly. She is stroking my hair.

"I didn't pull the trigger and hurt that boy, Josh, but I allowed it to happen. And even if I couldn't have stopped it, I am responsible."

She says, "We are all responsible for one another. Even people we don't yet know. It's like watching someone get bullied in school and not doing anything about it, just because you're scared. Or just because you don't want to get involved."

I can see from under my folded arms, all the way across the room, where Matoo standing by the vending machine. She's been there so long, pretending that she's trying to decide what she wants to eat. They don't let you just walk around in here, so she's got to look busy. I see her pulling one of those Cup-a-Soup out of the little door and going over to the microwave to warm it up.

My mother goes on, "You want to go along on your way, because that's the easier thing to do. And some people live their whole lives that way. And it works for them. But one day we'll all need someone, a stranger maybe. And you want to believe they will do the right thing."

I lift my head. "But you didn't?"

"No, I didn't," she says. "And an innocent boy lost his life."

"Josh Tipps?"

My mother nods her head. "And you. And I will never forgive myself for what I did to you either."

"But then you did do something? You stayed in the store with him. Why did you do that?"

"Why didn't I run? Like . . . like Nick did?"

She doesn't want to say his name out loud, I can tell. "Yeah."

"I hardly remember that night, Ruby. But when I realized what was happening, what was about to happen, it was like my eyes were forced open. The danger of the whole life I had been living, that *we* had been living, was so clear. And I hated myself in that moment. I would do anything, Ruby, to do it over again."

I see that she is trying hard not to cry, not to look weak, but to be strong, for me.

"But you didn't deserve that," she is saying. Her jaw is so tight. I want to reach out and touch her face. I want to make everything okay.

"You've had to pay the price for my mistake. And that will never be all right. And to think you even thought it was your new friend's brother. Aunt Barbara told me. That must have been awful. That must have been so awful. Ruby, I am so sorry."

Finally, Matoo comes back with two bottles of water and an apple juice for me. And three cheeseburgers and her Cup-a-Soup, all piping hot.

"I wish you could meet Margalit," I say.

"I know, sweetie. I feel like I have in a way. From your story. What did you name her in the story?"

"Moochie."

"Oh, right. Moochie. That's such a terrific name."

Maybe one day in the future, my mom will come home and meet Margalit in person. She could meet Margalit's mom. And Margalit's mom could bake those cookies. And my mom would see Loulou. And we'll be together. But it won't be soon. I know that now more than ever.

When my mother is released from prison I will be thirty-one years old.

That is way too far outside my brain for me to handle right now.

Right now we are having this delicious feast—I love these cheeseburgers—just the three of us. And for now, it is as right as we can make it.

Chapter Twenty-Five

It's not exactly like I am going to start my first day of sixth grade with a Facebook post about my mother being in prison or anything like that. But just knowing that Margalit is my best friend and that no one can take that away from me makes me feel a little less of a liar already.

Margalit confided to me that she was pretty nervous about starting a new school, and a middle school at that. But I assured her I was there to help. She has a Ruby Danes.

So we are all waiting at the bus stop. I haven't seen Kristin all summer and here she is.

"Hi, Ruby," she says. She can tell just by looking at me and Margalit that we are friends now. I am actually worried that it might hurt her feelings. That she might feel left out.

I mean, it's not like she wanted me for a best friend, but somehow I feel a bit like I should have told her before. Sometimes, people you think have it all, really don't. And you just never know, do you?

"Hi, Kristin," I say back. Margalit is waiting. "This is Margalit."

"I know that, silly," Kristin says. "I'm the one who told you who she was, remember?"

That didn't sound good. I think I am in one of those movies where the best friend finds out someone was paid to be her friend and when she finds out she runs off crying and it takes the whole rest of the movie to straighten things out.

But I forgot, this is Margalit.

"Oh, hi. Did you?" she says to Kristin. "I'm glad you did, or me and Ruby wouldn't have met. Do you live here too? I like your skirt."

And just like that, it's all okay.

The bus stops right to the beginning of the condo complex. So all the kids end up here at one time or another. Yvette and Beatrice would be long gone. High school starts at seven twenty-five. The real little kids, like we were last year, don't have to catch the bus for another hour and all their moms will wait with them. But there is an unspoken rule for the middle school: no parents. They have to wait at least fifty yards back or watch from their window if they live facing the street.

Matoo was a nervous wreck.

"But how will I know if you got on the bus safely?" she said while she was putting on her makeup, getting ready for work. She leaned her face toward the mirror and drew an outline of her lips.

"Where else would I be?"

She gave me that look. Matoo can come up with all kinds of worry. Better not to ask.

"I'll be fine," I told her. "It's a block away. And besides, I have Margalit."

I know Matoo wanted to sit in her car and wait for the bus, but she finally gave in.

"Oh hey, look at this," Kristin is saying. She takes something out of her backpack and holds it up. "My mother got me a smartphone."

It's so pretty. It's got a purplish cover with swirling pink flowers. And it surprises me but I'm not that jealous. A little, but not horribly.

I want Kristin to know that I have something new too. I have a best friend. A best friend who likes me no matter what. I have a Margalit. But what flies out of my mouth surprises us all. Most of all, me.

"The reason you never see my mother isn't because she's at work all the time, or traveling in Canada like I told you last year, Kristin."

Both Margalit and Kristin are paused in time. Neither of them moves or says anything.

"It's because my mother is serving time in Bedford Hills. She didn't do anything but she was with someone who did. And so if you want to judge me, Kristin, you can."

Margalit raises her eyebrows. And I've seen Loulou do that too. And then Kristin says, "Yeah, so what? I knew that."

I guess I'll never know if she did or she didn't, but it's done. But she doesn't really seem to be that interested.

But, of course, I could be wrong and Kristin will go to school and blab it all over, but either way it's out there in the universe and it doesn't seem nearly as bad as when it was threatening me from the inside. I have to face it sometime.

Why not now?

It might even make a good story for me to write one day.

Margalit, however, doesn't miss a beat. She just turns to Kristin and says, "Can I see your new phone?"

"Sure. Look, see you just wave your hand over it. And check out this app." Kristin is busy showing us this cartoon cat face named Tom that comes up on the screen and when you record something into the phone the cat face says it back to you in this funny kitty voice.

Kristin holds the phone to her mouth to show us again. "Hello there. I am going to school today. What are you doing?"

Sure enough, Tom the cat repeats everything word for word.

"Can I try?" Margalit says.

To my surprise Kristin hands over her phone. "Just be careful. It's brand-new."

"I got my ticket for the long way," she starts singing.

I join in, "The one with the prettiest of views. It's got mountains—"

And then Kristin does too. "It's got rivers. It's got sights to give you shivers!"

She must have learned the same song. Tom the cat blinks his eyes several times and then sings back our song in three voices. When the bus pulls up to the condo we are all still laughing, trying different songs, the Pledge of Allegiance, our names, what we had for breakfast.

All in all, it's pretty normal.